D1014654

Mr. and
Mrs. Baby

Mr. and Mrs. Baby

and other stories by

Mark Strand

Alfred A. Knopf   New York   1985

*This is a Borzoi Book
published by Alfred A. Knopf, Inc.*

"The General," "Two Stories," and "The Killer Poet" were
originally published in *Antaeus*.

"Zadar" originally appeared in the Summer 1984 *Michigan
Quarterly Review*.

"More Life," "The Tiny Baby," "True Loves," "Mr. and Mrs.
Baby," "Wooley," and "The President's Resignation" were
originally published in *The New Yorker*.

"Dog Life" was originally published in *Vogue* as
"The Dog Story."

Other stories have been previously published in *The Antioch
Review* and *Rolling Stock*.

Library of Congress Cataloging in Publication Data

Strand, Mark. [*date*]
  Mr. and Mrs. Baby and other stories.
  Contents: More life—True loves—The tiny baby—[etc.]
  I. Title. II: Mister and Mrs. Baby and other stories.
PS3569.T69M7 1985 813'.54 84-48509
ISBN 0-394-51359-2

*Manufactured in the United States of America
First Edition*

*To Chip McGrath
and Dan Halpern*

Contents

Mr. and
Mrs. Baby

More Life

SEVERAL YEARS AGO, HAVING JUST quit a job in a brokerage house which I'd held since graduating from business school, I went to Maine to visit a friend who had a summer house near Thomaston. My first days there it rained, and everything in the house smelled damp; outside, the landscape was dark and sodden. I was disappointed, depressed, and on the verge of leaving. Then, one morning, I rose and saw thin, broken clouds moving swiftly overhead. It was the end of the bad weather. The sun was out and the damp was lifting. By noon the sky was an endless, monotonous blue. In the late afternoon, my friend and I decided to go for a walk over the fields that covered the low hills to the west of his house. As we walked through a clearing bounded by the sea on one side and a jagged line of pine trees on the other, I thought of my father, who had been a writer, and who, when I was still a youngster, had moved the family from New York City to live in Maine. He was in his late thirties and had written only two novels; neither was well received. He was having trouble getting started on a third and blamed his failure on the distractions of city life. So we went to Maine. There were times, especially when we first moved there, when my mother and I were enchanted by the energy of my father. He paraded before us in his underwear, reading aloud from Rabelais, instructing us in boldness, in ardor, in pretense. He was the authority. Peering over his reading glasses, waving an index finger over his head, he preached domination of uncertainty, vagueness, despair. His boxer shorts began under his bulging belly and ended just above his knees; his calves were massive but hairless, and his ankles were as thin as a woman's. His parading was a kind of dance to the music of words. My mother and I sat together in a big chair, uplifted and amazed.

But there were times later on when my father's steps revealed his impatience, his mounting frustration. He had abandoned one novel and wanted to begin another. He blamed the quiet, the dullness of Maine for his inability to do so. His boredom made him nervous. He said he could feel within himself the exaggeration of moments, the lengthening of hours. He was perpetually on the threshold of beginning something but could not get beyond the initial impulse to sit and write. My mother and I would hear him pacing his room. He seemed to live in a marginal world between routine and transport, between laziness and desire. Day after day, he confronted the newspaper, the coffee, the attempt to write, the walk, the sea, the dinner, the wish to return to New York, the fear of doing so. He bought cases of over-the-hill wine on sale. He would drink and rave on about greatness. "More life, more life!" he would bellow. My mother urged him to get a teaching job, but he would not. He said he hated security, and claimed that immortality, not tenure, was a writer's business. But in ten years of living in Maine he did not finish one book. And eventually my mother ran off to live with the local doctor, and took me with her.

My friend had walked on ahead, while I stared into the summer twilight. Walking in a place so close to where we had lived not only allowed me to feel the poignancy of my father's failure but made it somehow inescapable. It saddened me that he died with no recognition at all. I'm not sure how long I stood in that field, but I began to feel a terrible stillness. The warm air seemed weighted with the perfume of summer. Then I heard a fly. It circled me once, and hovered before me at eye level, staring at me. Its metallic-green body glinted in the last rays of sunlight. Its buzzing increased and subsided rhythmically. The sound was threatening, yet there was something familiar about it, something that went beyond mere buzzing. This is hard to account for, but I was suddenly convinced that my father had returned. He had come back as a fly.

He buzzed and buzzed, and I was afraid that he'd bite if he landed on me. Yet I could not lift my hand against him. I fell to my knees. He resumed his noisy circling, broken by attacks in which he would swerve suddenly at my face, stop a few inches away, then continue to circle. "Dad!" I said. "Go ahead, land on me." His buzzing became extremely loud and suggested frantic disapproval. I remember wishing there were some way we could talk. He flew away. "Dad, don't leave," I yelled. "Come back." Perhaps I had been wrong, I thought. Perhaps he had come back not to harm me but to beg forgiveness—to abase himself before me as a simple fly. "Dad, you're innocent, you did nothing wrong," I called. Then I heard the buzzing again. He was back, but he was not alone. He had come with a buzzing swarm of friends. I got up and began to run. The next thing I knew, I was on my back and my friend was leaning over me, staring.

I never told my friend what had happened. I all but put the episode aside, never trusting it to the ears of anyone. And it wasn't until about a year later, when I was again bored with a job, that I thought very much about my father. Not about his awful transmogrification the summer before but about his life in New York, where he returned after my mother had left him. In those days, I would go down to New York and stay with my aunt and her husband. In the afternoons I would visit my father, who lived in a studio apartment with a makeshift kitchen at one end and his bed at the other. It was a cramped, book-crowded place, and when I went there he usually sat at his desk, which was in the center of the room, or lay on his back, staring at the ceiling. Once when I visited him, he recalled with theatrical emphasis "the dawn in Maine, the caw of crows lifting with the mist, the peeping and chirping of warblers, goldfinches, and catbirds." Then he looked at me sadly and said, "Charlie, tell me, why am I here? Why did I come back?" Another time, when I asked him how his work was going, he said that it wasn't. He told me that there was a novel he wanted to begin but couldn't. After all, he explained, what sphere was his? What did he know about any place or occupation? Nothing. His specialty was blankness, the features of boredom, the haze of habit. He said that his notes were of intangible states—the feel of sinking into sleep, of drifting into daylight. He confessed he had been lazy and lacking in purpose, that he had been an emotional drifter, that his grandiose determination to create a lasting attachment with something—anything— through his writing was fraudulent.

In the years just before he died, my father became a ladies' man. His age, his belly, his close-cropped hair in a time when everyone else's was long made him an unlikely Lothario, but he was a triumph, surpassing, at times, even his own windy expectations. He wooed with a wistfulness that won sympathy. He alluded to his life in Maine as if he were in exile from Arcady. He spoke of himself as a simple man, at home under Maine's great sky, with its store of mists, fogs, and clouds, its slanting maritime light. He described walks he took at dusk by the sea—its dark body turning and turning in its lace of seaweed and foam. But he also made it clear that life on the "stone coast" was not always easy, that his sensitive nature, if not directly imperilled, was under siege. He talked of sitting at night in a circle of soft light, reading a book, while outside the wind hissed through the trees and on the roof and against the windowpanes the loud pattering of rain began.

My own life in New York was dominated by routines that enlivened without necessarily giving pleasure. I spent hours each day on the phone, went to parties, drank, and watched television. There were several women I took out, but I was not in love with any of them. Sometimes they were secretaries who idolized me for the wrong reasons. Assuming the authority I affected at the office was genuine, they would relinquish themselves to my charge. Sometimes they were successful colleagues. I liked to think their self-assurance would rub off on me, but it never did. They were drawn to my vagueness, my uncertainty, my inability to come to terms with my life as it was unfolding. None of these relationships lasted. My one pleasure was horseback riding. I did it in the Park on weekends and holidays, and I rode with a zeal that bordered on the fanatic. I rode from every misfortune I could imagine —from my job, from the women I knew, from the sterility of my small apartment.

One autumn Saturday I was riding a sleek chestnut gelding with large, nervous eyes. A few leaves fluttered from the trees. The sky was bright, the air was dry, and everywhere there was a remarkable clarity. My horse moved cleanly, responding with ease to my commands. For an instant it occurred to me that this was the way the world should be, and that my unchallenged dominance over my mount would have pleased my father. Then, suddenly, as if to protest my arrogance, the horse stopped. I urged him forward, but he was stubborn. I began to rock in the saddle. Powerless and frustrated, I lost my composure. I called him an idiot and kicked my heels into his sides. He turned his head slowly to the left. He seemed to be watching something, following its motion. I looked up to see what it was. A woman was walking over one of the bridges that crossed the bridle path. She was tall and dark-haired and wore a light purple coat. She walked with an easy stride that suggested the possibility of physical abandon. I immediately dismounted and stood before the horse. I was sure he was my father. It made perfect sense —the horse was an ideal medium for him. In some indefinable way, they were alike. The horse gazed longingly, it seemed to me, after the disappearing woman, its eyes melting into tenderness, then despair.

"Dad," I said. "It's great to see you." He turned his head and watched another woman cross the bridge. Not far off an ambulance or police-car siren whined. I felt a chill. "Dad, don't worry. I won't ride you again. Everything will be all right." He looked beyond me, at the woman. "Dad," I went on, getting carried away, "I'll do whatever you want. I'll get you out of the stables and into the country. I'll buy a house in Connecticut; you can have the backyard all to yourself." He neighed and shook out his mane. I put an arm over his neck in a casual gesture of affection. "Dad, tell me that you'll let me help you, care for you, make life easy for you." At that point, my father reared and bolted. I stood in his dusty wake. There was no point in my trying to change his mind. Even as a horse he was headstrong.

Days passed in which I did nothing but consider the peculiarity of my father's behavior. I was afraid to go out for fear I would meet him again, and again be rebuffed. I brooded. I drank. I stared out the window. But the ordeal of loneliness became tiresome. I tried to resume my social life and to throw myself into my work, but failed. Upset and distracted, I found even the most routine tasks difficult. I lost faith in my ability and gave in to feelings of ennui and impotence.

It was several months before my life took on its normal flow. The incident with the horse slipped from memory, and I was happier than I had ever been before. For one thing, I had fallen in love. Her name was Helen Schulz.

She was a lawyer and lived in my building. I had been noticing her for months in the elevator. Her light blue eyes were heavily made up and looked almost yellow. Her dark eyebrows, however, preserved for them an intensity that would otherwise have been lost. She had high cheekbones and short auburn hair swept straight back. Her skin—at least when I saw her in the elevator—seemed to glow. But it was her eyes, on these occasions, that offered, with stunning insistence, the promise of sexual fulfillment. The brevity of our encounters meant that getting to know her was a long ordeal of suppressed elation, of waiting, of gaining courage.

The first time we had dinner together, I could barely eat. My stomach churned with excitement. She was even more beautiful in the restaurant than she had been in the elevator. There was about her a serenity and naturalness that set me at ease. Before long, we were spending all our free time together. She brought out the best in me. Our evenings together were filled with gaiety. We told each other stories of our past, sometimes with breezy offhandedness, sometimes with cautious solemnity. But, happy as we were, I felt that by not telling her about my father's reappearances I was lying to her. I wanted to tell her, and I felt I had to, but there never seemed to be an appropriate occasion. And I wasn't sure how she would respond.

Finally, at my apartment one night, the time seemed right. I sat on the floor; Helen sat across the coffee table from me, on the couch. She had a vitality that was delicate and precious, and that seemed, paradoxically, the issue of weariness. A certain heaviness of spirit made her radiance seem flickering and momentary. And then I realized I was not looking at Helen at all but at my father.

"Dad," I said, "you're back!"

"Darling," he said, "what is it? What's wrong?"

I could tell this had been one of his down days. He had given in to his gift for gloom. It was clear from the frown he wore that he considered his life a waste. I got on my knees in front of the coffee table. "Dad, Dad, you're too hard on yourself."

He reached for my hands. "What's come over you?" he said.

"Dad, it's you, it's you."

He must have been moved, for there were tears in his eyes and he seemed unable to speak.

"Dad, relax. There's nothing to worry about."

He stood up. "Charlie, dear, I'm frightened," he said.

"What of?" I said.

"Of you," he answered.

My father afraid of me? I was astonished. My father stood before me and spoke with the voice of a terrified woman. It was too much to bear. I closed my eyes and collapsed onto the couch. I felt grand. I felt as if I would burst into flame. There was a sudden thinness of air, a quiet that made the distance audible. For a moment I felt as though I encompassed the whole world. When I awoke, in my pajamas and under a blanket, I was alone.

Helen came over the next day to see how I felt. She stood in the heavy stream of morning light, looking more lovely than ever. I told her I hoped she was not upset by what had happened. She said she had been frightened but now was over it. She knelt beside me and explained that it made her realize how much she loved me.

I took her hands. "Helen," I said, "let's go to Maine. We'll walk by the sea. We'll trawl for mackerel and visit small islands." She stared at me. My sudden energy seemed to amuse her. "In the morning, we'll listen to warblers, goldfinches, and catbirds. At night, we'll build a fire."

"What's got into you?" she said.

"Nothing. Nothing at all," I said.

We went to Maine that summer, and the days were long and leisurely. My visions of the future were calm and untroubled. Helen and I decided to get married. And my father's visits were rare, if one could say they were visits at all. I'd stand in the bathroom, shaving, and catch a flicker of something out of the corner of my eye. I'd look at myself and feel him near me, his breath barely beginning to cloud the mirror. But it would last just a second.

True Loves

THIS IS A CONFESSION. I AM A MAN IN his mid-forties who has been married five times, and been in love six—always outside the bounds of matrimony. Not that I treated my wives badly—it was always my intention to shield them from emotional misfortune whenever possible. I wanted them to be happy. As my fearless succession of marriages proves, my faith in the institution was never shaken. Then why did my extramarital loves exceed the number of my marriages? Only because my loves were true loves! They caused me unheard of agony and, at the same time, pleasure of almost blinding incandescence. I offer the following glosses as testimony to them.

I shall spare you the details of what brought me to Machu Picchu, but it was there that I fell in love for the first time.

I was standing in the semi-enclosed, almost trapezoidal Sacred Plaza and staring westward into the awesome valley of the Urubamba, when I happened to turn and see an attractive woman dressed in a khaki outfit. It was modelled from boots to hat with considerable care, it seemed to me, on the costume Hiram Bingham was photographed in when he discovered Machu Picchu. She was looking not at me but at some terracing on the opposite side. I turned away and gazed again at the Urubamba, silver and serpentine, more than a thousand feet beneath me. When I turned back to the woman, she was gone.

I continued to explore, wandering among gray stone shells of houses whose thatched roofs had deteriorated centuries ago, climbing and descending the countless stairways that seemed to bind the town together. Then I saw her again. She was seated on a fallen lintel, resting. When I sat on the grass before her, exaggerating my own weariness in an attempt to establish rapport, she smiled, then took off her hat and casually shook out her hair. I was so overcome by the calm of her demeanor, the easy disposition of her limbs, her overall grace and confidence that I found it difficult to speak. We had hardly been together five minutes when she asked me if I would like to climb Huayna Picchu. "Yes," I replied, even though I was tired. "Yes, I'd love to," I continued. I would follow her anywhere, do whatever she told me.

She led the way, first over the saddle that connects Machu Picchu and Huayna Picchu, then up the winding slippery path that leads to the top of Huayna Picchu. The twelve-hundred-foot climb took us an hour and a half, and though the views became more and more spectacular, my gaze was fixed on my guide's perfectly shaped buttocks and on her legs, which, despite the disfiguring bulkiness of her breeches and puttees, were long and lean. I was falling in love and trying to keep up, at the same time.

Her name was Marvella and she was English. We stood in the afternoon light, watching the blue sky deepen into evening. I told her how old I was and that I was born in Fargo, North Dakota, and that I lived in New York and that my wife was divorcing me.

We sat together at dinner in the little hotel that adjoins the ruins. She told me she was returning to Lima early the next morning. I asked her what hotel she was staying at, and if she would mind my calling on her. Her eyes seemed to radiate softness. Yes, I could call on her.

When I returned to Lima, a few days later, I went to the Pension Ramus, where she was staying. The landlady, Señora Ramus, said she was not in; she was rarely in and was sometimes out all night. Señora Ramus did not approve. Jealous of whoever or whatever kept her away, I rushed off, feeling despondent.

I took a cab to the Plaza San Martin and walked to the Negro-Negro, a bar where they made the best Pisco sours in Lima. I drank, hoping to rid myself of desire. I wandered out into the cool mist and drizzle of the night, foolishly mumbling her name over and over to myself. And then, miraculously, she appeared, walking toward me, leaning on the arm of a tall, mustachioed, very handsome man. She was giggling, and of course paid no attention to anything happening around her. I walked by without stopping.

My second love budded, bloomed, and faded in the setting of the New York subway system. Each day I would take a train from the Upper West Side to the financial district, bringing a book with me. It was a period when the news did not interest me—a failing that contributed to my eventually losing my job. At any rate, during the time I speak of I would board the train, clutching a copy of Lawrence, and become a straphanger and read.

I was in the middle of *Sons and Lovers* when I fell in love. And my love seemed inevitable, for seated below me was a young woman also reading *Sons and Lovers*. She did not look up. There was no way to catch her eye, no way to let her know that I was reading the same book—that is, not without creating what might be a moment of awful embarrassment. I hovered above her, uncertain, not even knowing what she looked like, though I liked the simple, unaffected way she dressed—almost primly, in a light brown tweed skirt and a loose-fitting deep green pullover that covered all but the collar and edge of the cuffs of a white cotton blouse. And I couldn't fail to notice the lustre of her straight, shoulder-length auburn hair, or her slim legs, crossed in front of her with careless grace that hinted at something more—a serene knowledge of sex. I wished to speak to her. I longed for a quiet place where I could whisper to her of the miraculous sequence of moments, hours, years that had brought us together. I was convinced that destiny had created this occasion for us, but I could not speak. Panic seized me. At any stop she might leave the train and the moment that fate had chosen for us would be lost, irretrievable in the rushing crowds of the city. While I was musing on the possibility of such a trag- edy, she rose from her seat and began to move toward the door. I saw her face for the first time: her thin, perfectly straight nose, her pale lips, her vaguely sullen eyes, which seemed smudged with fatigue—beautiful hazel-green eyes, luminous, autumnal, bewitching. She walked out of the train without looking at me or the book I was carrying.

I was depressed for a week, prey to an increasing silence that ruled my inner life, ruined my outer one. In that short period of time my second wife and I drifted apart. The text of our lives was not being written so much as erased. Words spoken became whispers and were lost in the softness and silence of intervals, stories became formless, disjointed events that took on the wayward quality of dreams, and meanings floated ominously close to extinction, allowing themselves to be lured to the edge of thought. I was in love with another woman.

My work, which had ceased to interest me, now became painfully dull. But I continued to go to the office, each day entering the same subway where I had fallen in love less than two weeks earlier. I lived in hopes of encountering her again. I stood each day in the same part of the train, finished *Sons and Lovers,* and began *Women in Love.* Then I saw her again. She was seated below me, engrossed in *Women in Love.* It was as if fate had given us one more chance. How can I describe the nervous joy that came over me, the sweet excitement, the familiar yet unfathomable fear? There were her legs, crossed just as they had been, and the same shoes, and her lucent hair. Only her dress was different—her dress and *Women in Love.* There was even more to say than before, but I was unable to speak. I was shy, fearful of making a fool of myself, fearful of making a scene in case she didn't share my wonder at the coincidence of our reading the same Lawrence books at the same time and place. What was the matter with me? I was a grown man. I knew my way around.

Why this childish desperation? But what would I say? Would I have to bend down so that she might hear me? And would the sudden presence of my face mooning before her frighten her? Even when she got up and moved toward the door—again without so much as looking at me—I could not follow her. Instead, I stood my own meagre ground, filled with shame and mild self-loathing. Everything in me sank into despair as I watched her go. Whatever my accomplishments had been, they were suddenly meaningless. My hopes collapsed, for I knew that I would never see her again, that fate had given me two chances which a characteristic and overpowering timidity had spoiled. Within a month my wife left me. Within two months I was living in Los Angeles.

The third time I fell in love was at a dinner party in Hollywood. Though she was a famous actress, I cannot name her, for doing so would reduce our moments of painful intimacy to mere boasting. She was beautiful. Her eyes were almost black, and seemed at times bottomless in their inviting depths and at other times so opaque that their gaze, instead of engaging the object in their line of vision, stopped short and returned to dwell on what was within. They were deeply set under eyebrows that were strong and perfectly arched. When I first saw her, she was seated in the yellowish glow of a lamp, leaning back on a heavily pillowed sofa. Her beauty seemed shadowy and elusive; she spoke to no one. For me, it was an unbearable scene of noble, polished, studied isolation. Her grand ease made me timid; I wanted more than anything to sit beside her, to bask in her self-containment. Not possible. We were called to dinner by our hosts.

She sat across from me, so I had further opportunity to study her, though still no chance of talking with her. Others spoke to her, but only for short periods; she never seemed part of the chatter that rose and fell in insignificant waves throughout dinner. I watched her mouth and it seemed always composed, always perfect. She chewed her food without a hint of vulgarity, her face retaining its magnificent calm. Then I noticed her white forearms, their faint, soft, silky, barely visible covering of hair, and the few pale veins almost concealed by the milky translucence of her skin. I was beginning to tremble, becoming disoriented. Her rings fascinated me; her nails, which were not too long, or polished, indicated that she was modest in ways not impossible to discover. I wanted to reach over and break through the forbidden radiance in which she dwelled. Nothing said at dinner could distract me for a second.

When we went into the living room for coffee and brandy, I sat beside her. The others stood, talking in small clusters, and we were alone. Aware of the relative quiet that engulfed us, I imagined we were being drawn together as two people in a ship's bar might be. I felt myself responding to the most minute suggestions of intimacy. I wanted to speak, but seemed mired in inadequacy as I watched the shape of her long thighs pressing against the sheer voile of her dress. I fumbled. I felt a certain boyish excitement in my pursuit of her. It seemed to me that her breath was quickening, a signal perhaps of reciprocal feelings. Her breasts heaved slightly. "I think you are beautiful," was all I could say. She leaned over to get her drink and I caught the odor of almond and the rapid sheen of light passing over the silky fall of her hair. "My God," I murmured to myself. Then I asked her if there was a chance I might see her again. The look in her eyes seemed to suggest there was. Her lips played with the rim of her glass. I was desperate, out of control. I began saying one silly thing after another, beginning with "I don't like dinner parties," and ending with "I have to go to Australia." She sighed, but whether with pity or disappointment I could not say.

The next day I called my wife, who was visiting her mother in Chicago, and told her what had happened. She made it clear that she never did trust me, that she would not return, and that I should send her belongings out to her mother's.

What I had told the movie actress about my going to Australia was true. I went as a bank representative to Sydney and married for the fourth time—something my diminutive Australian wife did not find out until we were several months into our marriage. It was a mark of my discretion that I chose the positive virtue of silence over the negative one of truth. But efforts to shield my new wife from the mistakes of my past did not help establish a firm relationship. Our marriage was dull and our schemes, our elaborate inventions for creating excitement always ended in failure. Our leisure time seemed like an exaggeration of itself—banal, bleak, grievously long. Last, and most important, I had a physical yearning for more than my wife's tiny frame cound endure.

It was at a cocktail party in fashionable Paddington that I met Wanda. Wanda. The very name still strikes a chord of magical passion within me. Wanda the immense, Wanda the voluptuous, who told me soon after we met ond bottle of Lindeman's, which we drank until the rain stopped and the yellow glow of twilight flooded the room.

We said nothing on the drive back. The craving I felt on the way out had given way to a slumberous sense of well-being. Through half-closed lids I watched Wanda's face become intermittently bright in the glare from the lights of oncoming traffic. When she dropped me off, we sat in her car for a minute or two without speaking, draped in the dark of the Sydney night. I wanted to lean over and kiss her, to thank her, to tell her I longed to see her again and again. She must have understood, for she sighed and then, with discretional wisdom, said, "Good night, love." That was the last I saw of Wanda in the flesh, although for months and months I would see her in my dreams, nude or semi-clothed, driving me to and from Berowra Waters Inn, where we ate that day.

Less than a week after our lunch I received word from the bank's New York office that I was to return to the United States for reassignment. My petite wife wanted to stay in Sydney, and, in fact, the moment I left filed formal separation papers. I never saw her again and have never been back to Australia.

The next time I fell in love was on a late October Sunday morning in Halifax, Nova Scotia. I was walking north on Barrington Street and she was walking south. The air had a glassy brilliance, a clarity about it, a dryness unusual in that part of the world. Yet it held the familiar odors of pine and the sea and traces, here and there, of burnt leaves. It would be a perfect day. As I watched the woman approach, I noticed she was watching me and that her steps became a little tentative, the swinging of her light

that when she made love her hair fell out; immediately a
certain giddiness came over me and I rose into that airy
region of love. Never had anyone—one tends to forget
one's previous loves—seemed more desirable. I wanted to
tell her, wanted to thrust myself on her, but I was afraid.
The wonderful Wanda, her eyes like coals in her moony
visage, looked at me, understanding my reticence.

The next day she met me at work and drove me to
lunch in her blue Alfetta. We rode in driving rain, through
Turramurra and Warrawee. "Where are we going?" I
asked, wanting to rest my hand on her thigh. "You must
be starved, love," she said, suddenly turning and smiling
at me. How I adored her then, how I wished she would
pull the car to the side, how I wanted to drown myself in
the pink sea of her flesh!

"We're getting close," she said.

"Not close enough," I replied ambiguously.

When she parked the car, we dashed through the rain
down some battered concrete steps and into a small waiting ferry that took us across the Hawkesbury River.

Wanda. Wanda. Under that cloud-darkened sky, those
drifting curtains of rain, your blond abundance filled our
tiny boat with light. And in the restaurant, as we looked
out over the gray water to the streaked outcroppings of
rock and the gum trees, with their leaves in sad, falling
bouffant clusters, what lightness of heart I experienced.
How far away the rest of my life seemed as we sipped our
Lindeman's Hunter River Burgundy and slowly ate our
hot salad of duck livers with raspberry vinegar. I cannot
recall what we talked of, but the sweet serenity of that
meal still lingers; how easily we submitted ourselves to the
filet of beef in Bordelaise sauce with marrow, and a sec-

gray flannel skirt less rhythmical. She suddenly looked away, turned, and crossed the street. I watched her as she resumed her stride. She wore a tan Harris tweed jacket, and her short but straight brown hair bounced slightly as she walked. She turned her head to watch me as we passed each other. I saw that her eyes were tender, inquisitive. For a moment it seemed that each of us might stop and address the other. But we continued on our ways. I loved the easiness, the lightness of her walk and the moment of hesitancy before she crossed the street. It was perfectly right that she did cross. To have passed each other close by might have been unbearable; she obviously knew this. I continued up Barrington Street, lost in a reverie of her. Then I stopped and looked around, and the world for an instant assumed a deep benevolence that was strangely charged and that lifted me from the possibility of resignation, numbness, or despair. I turned and headed south, in the direction I had just come. It was still early and the surrounding silence seemed enormous, as if the world were holding its breath for a momentous occurrence.

She, too, had turned around, for I saw her on the opposite side, heading toward me. Again we stared at each other. Her gaze had softened and seemed pleased to take me in. Her mouth formed a slight smile, understated and tentative, but she walked by and did not stop. I stood, watching her, knowing that she would return to me, that for her to have stopped just then, as I had, would have been premature, that having passed me again to return once more would be ample proof of her love. Several blocks later, she turned abruptly and headed in my direction. My heart beat wildly, my body ached with sudden tension. We stood across from each other. Again she smiled, but conspiringly. This was the purest, briefest, most complete of all my loves. The air was filled with the heat of containment; it shimmered with possibility. It was by tacit consent that we kept our distance, to give the flame of our passion ample space. We walked back and forth on Barrington Street until the presence of others made it impossible for us to stop and to stare. By mid-morning we had each gone our own way.

Within two months I had married for the fifth time. She was a Yugoslav who knew little English and liked dancing.

My marriage to Jasmina did not last long. I liked Belgrade despite its grayness, and liked sitting in front of the Hotel Moskva, reading four-day-old *Herald Tribunes,* but Jasmina drove me insane, dragging me from one dancing place to another. I decided to run away.

Planes from Belgrade at that time of year were often cancelled because of fog, but even in clear weather they could not be relied on. Thus my escape to Venice would be accomplished by train. I picked a night when my wife was out with her friends, threw my clothes into a suitcase, grabbed two bottles of wine, and ran to the station, just a few blocks from our tiny apartment in the heart of the city.

By the time the train pulled out, I was already sipping some of the wine. I stood in the corridor in front of my small sleeping compartment, which had already been made up, and felt a great sense of relief. Zagreb, Ljubljana, Trieste, Venice—Jasmina would never find me, would probably not try. My compartment mate was a Rumanian computer engineer who had been on board since Bucharest and was headed for Rome. He told me he had spent a few months in the United States, in Poughkeepsie. As he made this disheartening admission, a woman walked out of the next compartment and stood beside us. When my friend introduced us, he said that she, too, was travelling from Bucharest, to visit her sister in Genoa. Her name was Sylvia. She seemed nervous, a bit wary, but charming, and eager to hear whatever I said.

I offered both my companions some wine. He declined. She accepted, but with a lustiness that made me uneasy. She emptied her glass, then emptied another, and another. I opened the second bottle. Our conversation became animated despite the limitations of her English. We named our favorite movies, then movie stars; we listed our favorite cities and restaurants; she wanted to know where the best beaches in America were. At this point, my roommate, apparently tired of listening to our conversation, announced that he was going to bed. As soon as he closed the compartment door, Sylvia asked me if I thought American women were sexy. We were alone in the corridor. I was suddenly breathless; my pulse quickened, I felt overcome by the renewal of long-lost joy. Sylvia's brown eyes were looking straight into mine. She was dark and her black hair lay heavily on her slight shoulders. I watched her shift her weight. She had beautiful legs and wide, inviting hips. Then, looking back into her eyes, I told her that American women were not in a class with Rumanians or Yugoslavs. I poured myself another glass and told her I thought *she* was sexy. Instantly, I regretted having done so. Her face changed and she assumed a demeanor of stricken, frenzied awareness. Suddenly she tossed her head and looked away from me. Did I love her? I think so. Did she love me? I think not. "How could you say dat!" she said, turning toward me again, her eyes brimming with accusatory tears. I told her that I loved the Rumanic roll of her vowels, her great sensitivity, that her soul was what I found sexy, but she didn't understand my English. I offered her some more wine; she put her hand over her glass. I poured some for myself, hoping to drown my embarrassment. "Please forgive me," I said, forcing a hurt look into my eyes. "I forgive," Sylvia said, coquettishly tilting her head to one side and smiling. But there was no way to recapture the innocent flow our conversation had had. We became silent. Finally, we said good night and went to our separate compartments.

I found it hard to sleep. I kept thinking of Sylvia, how different she was. Her darkness seemed to float in the dusk of my half-sleep. I imagined her whispering to me, the irresistible syllables of her broken English floating nakedly into my ears. Then I imagined her lips on mine. Then I would wake and stare at the ceiling and slowly drift back to sleep and to Sylvia. All night I moved dreamily in and out of her arms.

At six, when I was awakened by the border guards wanting to see my passport, I discovered my roommate already dressed and sitting on the edge of his lower berth. Sylvia was gone.

As I write this, I am living in Rome, and spend most of my time in a bar on the Via Frattina, staring at passers-by. Soon I shall have to return to the United States and go back to work, but right now I am content doing nothing. I think often of Sylvia and her inexplicable disappearance, but I don't let it torture me. My sights are set on the future. I see myself at a dinner party in Minneapolis, surrounded by Swedes and Norwegians, or walking along the lakefront in Chicago, the wind howling, the waves crashing, or standing in a bakery in New Haven, the smells of fresh rye bread and cinnamon rolls coming together. Of course, there is no telling what will happen. At any moment my plans could be altered.

The American couple at the next table have been discussing their recently divorced daughter, waiting for her to join them. But nothing in their concern has prepared me for the tall, fashionably dressed woman who seems to appear from nowhere and sits down with them, her red hair falling over her shoulders in loose, almost dishevelled curls. And I am struck by her rich tan, which I would have thought was her natural color but for the pearly white of her underarms. Her attitude is casual, even languid, as she leans back and takes a long, easy drag on her cigarette, and her eyes are sullen and mistrustful. Clearly, she is my type. And I can see that under her calm exterior she is passionate, barely in control of needs that must be driving her even at this moment, without her knowing, ever closer to me, and that I am ready once again to fall in love, or perhaps get married.

The Tiny Baby

Even before the baby was born, its mother hired a sitter to prepare for the days when she'd need one. She told the sitter, "The baby's in the living room, but it's real small. If you don't see it, don't worry." Then the mother pretended to leave, and hid in the bushes outside the living-room window, watching the sitter's every move. The tiny baby was so tiny that its mother never looked pregnant. And when it was born, it took a long time for the doctor to find it. If it had wings, it would have been a goldfinch or a chickadee. Primitives in the community who heard of the tiny baby joked that it was small because its father was far away. "Like a dot on the horizon," they said. The mother feared for the tiny baby, feared it would see every carpeted room as a prairie strewn with monuments, huge and upholstered, every tree as a green net of frangible light, every flower as a wound in the air. So she dressed the baby in a cat suit, with the soft gray stripes of a tabby, and sat in the afternoon sun, watching it bound and roll in the grass. Soon she doubted that such a deception would ensure the baby's safe passage into adulthood. She worried about the blades of grass, the thorns of bushes, the tumultuous advances of weather, to say nothing of the advances—caterwauling, indiscreet, brutishly fickle—of the neighborhood toms. The tiny baby's mother shuddered. She thought of removing the cat suit but did nothing until the baby killed a mouse. Then the suit came off. As everyone knows, a mother's love for her child lives in that lush conjunction of selfless concern and undisguised identification. It rises above chance in its easy and expert acceptance of duty. Its destiny extends beyond the mute scrutiny of Eros. Nothing compares with it. By contrast, the formal shenanigans that pass between a man and a woman are the mere stuff of comedy. The mother of the tiny baby obeyed the transcendent obligations of her sex with unalterable devotion. She tied the baby to the tail of a kite but never let go of the string; she kept the baby in her purse so she wouldn't lose it. At home, she put the baby in a little chair on the dining-room table, surrounded by roses. Would the tiny baby become a Hollywood star, spreading its light in every room? Would it rise to the top of Australian society? Would it join the Mormon Church, sit in the celestial room, and be reproduced, by mirrors, into eternity? It is well to consider the fortunes of the loved. They move through the splendors of hotel lobbies, they hang around pools in desert resorts, they read bestsellers in subways and trains. They are never alone. Now, consider the tiny baby years hence. A smallish woman with blue, beady eyes, watching the street for a sight of her favorite hairdo. When she sees it—the long black tresses forming a castle of hair—she will imagine it on herself. She sits in a flower-print dress. Her thin legs crossed, the tips of her shoes hardly reaching the ground, she suddenly, in barely audible tones, sings a song about rain falling and a man on a bicycle, hurrying home. The man's wife leans from a window, watching him, but is distracted by the noisy appearance of sea gulls. The smallish woman gets up. The train has left. The day keeps echoing around her. Everything is priceless, she thinks. Death will not have me. That is the story of the tiny baby.

The President's
Resignation

Eᴀʀʟʏ ᴛʜɪꜱ ᴇᴠᴇɴɪɴɢ ᴛʜᴇ ᴘʀᴇꜱɪᴅᴇɴᴛ
announced his resignation. Though his rise to power was
meteoric, he was not a popular leader. He made no prom-
ises before taking office but speculated endlessly about the
kind of weather we would have during his term, sometimes even making a modest prediction. And when, as it
happened from time to time, his prediction was not borne
out, he would quickly conceal his disappointment. His
critics accused him of spending too much energy on such
exercises, and were especially severe about his wasting
public funds on a National Museum of Weather, in whose
rooms one could experience the climate of any day anywhere in the history of man. His war on fluorocarbons,
known as the "gas crusade," is still talked about with
astonishment. Among those attending the President's

farewell address were: the First Minister of Potential Clearness & husband, the Warden of Inner and Outer Darkness & husband, the Deputy Chief of Lesser Degrees & wife, the First Examiner of Ambiguous Customs & two secretaries, the Chief of Transcendent Decorum & friend, the Assistant Magistrate of Exemplary Conditions & two friends, the Under-Secretary for Devices Appropriate to Conditions Unspecific & mother, the Lord Chancellor of Abnormal Silences & father, the Deputy Examiner of Fallibility and Remorse & daughters, the Chief Poet Laureate and Keeper of Glosses for Unwritten Texts & follower.

THE PRESIDENT'S
FAREWELL ADDRESS

Ladies and Gentlemen, friends and colleagues, thank you for coming this evening. I know how difficult for you the past few days have been and how sad you must be tonight. But I came to the presidency from the bottom of my heart and leave it with the best will in the world. And I believe I have weathered my term without betraying the trust of the people. From the beginning I have preached melancholy and invention, nostalgia and prophecy. The languors of art have been my haven. More than anything I wished to be the first truly modern President, and to make my term the free extension of impulse and the preservation of chance.

(Applause)

Who can forget my proposals, petitions uttered on behalf of those who labored in the great cause of weather—

measuring wind, predicting rain, giving themselves to whole generations of days—whose attention was ever riveted to the invisible wheel that turns the stars and to the stars themselves? How like poetry, said my enemies. They were right. For it was my wish to make nothing happen. Thank heaven it has been so, for my words would easily have been wasted along with the works they might have engendered. I have always spoken for what does not change, for what resists action, for the stillness at the center of man.

(Applause)

Thus we have been privileged to celebrate fifty-one national holidays, the fifty-one days I hesitated before taking office—the glorious fifty-one that now belong to the annals of meditation. How lovely the mind is when overcast or clouded with indecision, when it goes nowhere, when it is conscious, radiantly conscious, of its own secret motions.

(Applause)

And the hours spent reading Chekhov aloud to you, my beloved Cabinet! The delirium of our own unimportance that followed! How we sighed and moaned for the frailty of our lives! Not to be remembered in two hundred years, or even in two! And the silence that was ours, each of us overtaken with a feeling of moments prolonged, magically chronicled in the stillness of windows beyond which the minute changes of the world went on.

(Applause)

Friends, how can I tell you what weather has meant! The blue sky, its variations and repetitions, is what I look back on: the blues of my first day in office, the blues of my fifth day, the porcelain blues, the monotonous blues, the stately blues, the ideal blues and the slightly less than ideal blues, the yellow blues on certain winter days. Always the great cupola of light, a vague yet luminous crown, spread with tireless regularity, turning the prose of my life into exultation and desire. And then it would dim into twilight and the green edge of the world would darken. Finally the weather of night would arrive, under which I drifted as if my bed were a ship—the monstrous openness of night, in which birds become lost, in which sounds travel with a melancholy beyond tears, in which my dreams of a golden age seem, for a moment, diminished and hopelessly exiled. I have sailed and sailed my whole life.

(Applause)

I remember each morning, when I was young, setting out to cross the plains of boredom, over which small islands of shadow drifted according to the caprice of clouds. Little did I know that those days had historical importance. Airy monuments, blurred remembrances were being built, suggested, removed almost in the instant of their occurrence. Each morning, crossing those plains, armed only with desire for sympathy and adulation, I was even then forming the role I would play as President. The emptiness of those days was relentless and unfathomable as the breathing of parents. When would the world awake and acknowledge its light, that airy gold in which strange domes of gray paraded soundlessly, far off?

(Applause)

I have never ceased looking up at the sky and I never shall. The deep azures and ultramarines of disappointment and joy come only from it. The blessings of weather shall always exceed the office of our calling and turn our words, without warning, into the petals of a huge and inexhaustible rose. Thank you and goodbye.

Under Water

I DIVE INTO THE COLD LAKE AND SINK
through beams of sunlight to the dark terraces of the bottom. I close my eyes and suddenly it is morning. I smell
butterscotch pudding cooling on a shelf in the kitchen of
my aunt's house in Jollymore. Outside, the immense
bushes sway. A storm is approaching. The light is broken,
spread, and lost in the small leafy chambers of the trees
behind my mother, who wears a wide-brimmed hat shading
her eyes. The striped canvas deck chair beside her has a
canopy with little white tassles hanging down. My mother's dark hair is gathered in a bun. She holds my sister and
me on her lap. Her eyes are dark and dark-rimmed and
there is no hint of sadness in them. In front of the house I
see a small woman struggling up the sidewalk. She is on
crutches. Her shiny braces click and scrape the cement.

Her blouse is patched with sweat. I am afraid; afraid of her; afraid of the dwarf—her huge head and short limbs, her quick manly stride—who lives with two friends of my mother's. I am afraid she wants to marry me. In the rippled glass of my bedroom window I see the faces of monsters. I see the dwarf trying to get in. I hear the clicking of the paralytic's braces. Early one morning, I walk into my parents' bedroom. They are naked. My mother's hand rests on my father's thigh. She sees me and quickly removes her hand. Later, I strut into the maid's room. I have snipped some hair from my head and Scotch-taped it to my armpits. I try to wrestle her down but she is too strong. I come into the kitchen and overhear my mother and a friend in the living room talking about me. The woman says that I am slow for my age, that I should be looked at by a doctor. My mother says that I am big for my age and only seem slow. I tell my parents that I am going to visit a friend. When I get to his house I am afraid to ring the doorbell. I lie down in the adjacent field and every so often lift my head to see if there are signs of movement within the rooms. Finally, I go home and tell my parents I played with him. My parents find out that I didn't. When I am fourteen my mother encourages me to take out girls. I have nothing to say to them. I close myself up in a room and paint self-portraits. Each is more detailed than the last. I look so hard at myself in the mirror that I see nothing. My father stands in his white linen double-breasted suit. One hand is in his jacket pocket, the other holds a cigarette. My mother is on his arm. She wears a white dress and smiles almost girlishly, but in her eyes there is a little cloud, a touch of melancholy, as if she were looking into a future that promised nothing. Their intimacy is frail and the white light of afternoon washes over them and away. One morning in Connecticut, I lean out from the broken door of a greenhouse. I wear chinos and desert boots and a black sweater with a big collar. My hair is long and barely out of my eyes. The girl I am looking at is far away. She is someone I am looking for, someone I cannot make out. Minutes before my marriage I am playing solitaire and win. I take this as a serious omen not to get married. My father has been watching but says nothing until we are downstairs on the way to the courthouse. "You don't have to go through with it," he says. My wife says that my family spends lots of time in preparation for going out. We stand, all of us, in front of a big mirror, checking ourselves and saying that we look good. She thinks we are larger than life. We are actually smaller and live in hopes of getting larger. My wife is unhappy and thinks I should leave. She stands by the window while the sinking sun streaks her hair with orange and turns her face, even her blue eyes, golden. I hit the interstate, driving through silent fields, endless and black, through small towns where the only lights on are bare bulbs in single rooms or streetlamps shining on piles of trash. I drive all night and see only one man, an insomniac or alcoholic, waiting for the morning star to fade or the liquor store to open. In early April my mother dies of a heart attack. I arrive just in time for the funeral. My father dies after announcing that he would do so.

I sink through the watery dark toward the shifting, waving gardens of the bottom. I do not open my eyes. It is already afternoon and there is a turkey roasting in the kitchen of my aunt's house in Chosica. Condors pass overhead, slowly flapping their wings. The air is harsh and dry. I play in a cardboard box on the grass in front of my father who sits in a striped canvas deck chair. I tell him I am sailing away. He waves goodbye. In the desert sand near Lima my parents are sitting and laughing. My father wears a white cap and dark glasses. My mother is bareheaded and the wind blows strands of her hair across her face. Early one morning I walk into my parents' bedroom. They are naked. My mother's hand rests on my father's thigh. He sees me and jumps up. My mother pulls the covers over her head. I run from the scene. Later I am in bed with the maid, swimming helplessly on her enormous body. When she laughs, I bounce in the air. At Pacha-camac I stand in the niche of a reconstructed building. I hold my straw hat in one hand and a staff in the other. My shirt is outside my pants and I wear boots that come to mid-calf. My pockets bulge with teeth I have picked from the skulls that lie everywhere in shallow graves. In Bar-ranquilla it is so hot that I lie on the tile floor immediately after I shower. A puddle of water forms around me. I look at my shoes in the closet. They are green with mold. I lie with Laura in the camellia-scented garden. I put a hand between her thighs and inch up. She does nothing. I say I'm sorry. She says she wanted to cry. In Rio I work in a zoo where the penguins die like flies. I lean from the broken door of the lion house. I wear shorts and a pale blue shirt with a white collar. My hair is long and sun-streaked. The girl I am looking at is nowhere near but I think I know what she looks like. The lions begin to roar. I am on a bus that travels the road along the beach. I meet Sarah, the only other passenger. She has a long nose and dark dishevelled hair. She has thin ankles. We talk. We walk on the beach. In less than an hour we are making love. Later I tell her she must meet my parents. I tell her about the time I saw them standing together. I say that my father stood in his white linen double-breasted suit. One hand was in his jacket pocket, the other held a cigarette. My mother was on his arm. She wore a white dress and smiled wearily. In her eyes there was a touch of mirth, as if she were pretending at that moment to be happy. I tell her there was something in the light of that afternoon that was ominous. We are together almost a year, then she goes to Greece and I never see her again. Though some time later a friend tells me that when he was on the beach at Taormina, he saw her. Some people in a big yacht came by and anchored there; one of the people who didn't swim but stayed on deck to drink was Sarah. She was heavy, he says. I am propped up in bed, staring at the pale green hospital walls and listening to the monotonous traffic in the corridor just outside my room. Snow falls, disfiguring the bushes and parked cars. I feel I have lost the desire to go on. A long trapezoid of sunlight moves off the bed next to mine and slowly onto the wall, itself in some ways like an interval, an absence in the otherwise continual stream of events. When I am well I marry. I get a job with a bank. We move to St. Croix and are plagued by waterbugs that tumble into our room through a tear in the screen. All the next day my wife smokes and drinks coffee. There is a troubled look on her face. She does not like the sight of the submarine that keeps cruising around in the bay we see from our house. She is bored and leaves. One of her friends visits me. Her legs are an elegant version of my father's and she is blond like him. She says she is married. I say as far as I know I am too. The excitement is unbearable. A few days later my father dies of a heart attack. I climb the rocks at Peggy's Cove. The sea heaves its black-green body close to mine. I am frozen with wind-driven spray. Soon I am flying south.

I am sinking, not as I thought I would, but slowly, more slowly than the word "sinking" could ever imply, and I seem to be moving further away from my life. Everything changes. Maybe my mother is right when she says to one of her friends, The kid is a monster. Her friend is sitting on the couch, stark naked, drinking so heavily that though she tries several times to stand, she cannot. I'd like to take you home with me you cute little monster, she says. My mother staggers over to the woman and slaps her. In the sandbox with the little girl next door, I fall and get a splinter in my palm. Wanting to be brave, I try not to cry. Still, the tears come and I rush inside. When my mother asks me if I want a big Band-Aid or a small, I choose the small, but as soon as I see the girl I realize my mistake. I am ashamed I made such a fuss over what will look like a small wound. I enter the maid's room and tell her to look out, then I lunge and miss her entirely. I am going to stick you in the icebox, she says. I'm going to cut you up into little pieces and feed you to your parents. Only your father will know because he has such well-developed taste-buds. His tongue is long and sensitive and when it's out he never bumps into anything. If you ask me, his tongue is a masterpiece, it's better than a set of eyes. In the school-yard everyone says shazam and gets down on their stom-achs, moving their arms in a furious breaststroke. I believe I am different. I leap from the classroom window and break both legs. My parents are having a party downstairs.

I pretend I am sleepwalking, parading back and forth on
the landing, with my arms outstretched in front of me. On
the observation deck of the Empire State Building where
we've gone to celebrate my thirteenth birthday, my father
tells me that he is getting old. He stands in dungarees,
T-shirt, and light jacket. One arm holds me to him, the
other hangs down. We are laughing in the late afternoon of
one of those rare cloudless July days. He is laughing so
hard his eyes are closed and his mouth is wide open. I
comb the shores of the Hudson for stones crusted with
garnets. River rats scurry around me, their long tails slip-
ping over the stones. My mother says I should take out
girls, but I close myself in a room and paint self-portraits.
I work in the city hospital for contagious diseases, in the
polio ward, brushing the teeth of the totally paralyzed,
giving them baths, telling them stories, lifting their children
up to their faces to be kissed, cleaning their bedpans,
dressing their bed sores. One of the nurses says I can
sleep with her if I tell her I love her. Just tell me you love
me, she says. A woman calls to say she is delivering a
present from a friend. She tells me her room number at
the hotel. I rush right over. She greets me in a kimono
that is open. I am astonished that my friend would think
of such a present. Minutes before my marriage I am playing
solitaire and win. My father has been watching but says
nothing until we are downstairs on the way to the courthouse. You don't have to go through with it, he says. Soon
after my marriage, my mother dies. My wife and I spend
a summer in Italy. She is sunning herself on the terrace of
the house just outside Perugia. Across the valley Assisi
shines in the brilliant noonlight. A rat scampers, squeek-
ing, right by my wife, who jumps up and runs into the

house. My father is dying. I stand by the bed, looking down on his ashen face. He is asleep. I walk to the window. There is a regatta out on the bay. The sails poke up up from the blue sheets of water the way a handkerchief does from a pocket. Perhaps I should wave goodbye, perhaps I should not go home. When I turn to my father, the doctor is standing beside him, saying he's dead. I shall not go back, I say to the doctor. I shall rise from my watery sleep. I shall come to the surface and wake in the dazzle of a million tiny burning cradles.

Dog Life

GLOVER BARLETT AND HIS WIFE TRACY lay in their king-size bed under a light blue cambric comforter stuffed with down. They stared into the velvety, perfumed dark. Then Glover turned on his side to look at his wife. Her golden hair surrounded her face, making it seem smaller. Her lips were slightly parted. He wanted to tell her something. But what he had to say was so charged that he hesitated. He had mulled it over in private; now he felt he must bring it into the open, regardless of the risks. "Darling," he said, "there's something I've been meaning to tell you."

Tracy's eyes widened with apprehension. "Glover, please, if it's going to upset me, I'd rather not hear. . . ."

"It's just that I was different before I met you."

"What do you mean 'different'?" Tracy asked, looking at him.

"I mean, darling, that I used to be a dog."

"You're putting me on," said Tracy.

"No, I'm not," said Glover.

Tracy stared at her husband with mute astonishment. A silence weighted with solitude filled the room. The time was ripe for intimacy; Tracy's gaze softened into a look of concern.

"A dog?"

"Yes, a collie," said Glover reassuringly. "The people who owned me lived in Connecticut in a big house with lots of lawn, and there were woods out back. All the neighbors had dogs, too. It was a happy time."

Tracy's eyes narrowed. "What do you mean 'a happy time'? How could it have been 'a happy time'?"

"It was. Especially in autumn. We bounded about in the yellow twilight, excited by the clicking of branches and the parade of odors making each circuit of air an occasion for reverie. Burning leaves, chestnuts roasting, pies baking, the last exhalations of earth before freezing, drove us practically mad. But the autumn nights were even better: the blue lustre of stones under the moon, the spectral bushes, the gleaming grass. Our eyes shone with a new depth. We barked, bayed, and babbled, trying again and again to find the right note, a note that would reach back thousands of years into our origins. It was a note that if properly sustained would be the distilled wail of our species and would carry within it the triumph of our collective destiny. With our tails poised in the stunned atmosphere, we sang for our lost ancestors, our wild selves. Darling, there was something about those nights that I miss."

"Are you telling me that something is wrong with our marriage?"

"Not at all. I'm only saying that there was a tragic dimension to my life in those days. You have to imagine me with a friend or two on the top of a windswept knoll, crying for the buried fragments of our cunning, for the pride we lost during the period of our captivity, our exile in civilization, our fateful domestication. There were times when I could detect within the coarsest bark a futility I have not known since. I think of my friend Spot; her head high, her neck extended. Her voice was operatic and filled with a sadness that was thrilling as she released, howl by howl, the darkness of her being into the night."

"Did you love her?" Tracy asked.

"No, not really. I admired her more than anything."

"But there were dogs you did love?"

"It's hard to say that dogs actually love," said Glover.

"You know what I mean," said Tracy.

Glover turned on his back and stared at the ceiling. "Well, there was Flora, who had a lovely puff of hair on her head, inherited from her Dandie Dinmont mother. She was teeny, of course, and I felt foolish, but still. . . . And there was Muriel, a melancholic Irish Setter. And Cheryl, whose mother was a long-coated Chihuahua and whose father was a cross between a fox terrier and a shelty. She was intelligent, but her owners made her wear a little tartan jacket which humiliated her. She ran off with a clever mutt—part puli, part dachshund. After that I saw her with a black and white Papillon. Then she moved, and I never saw her again."

"Were there others?" said Tracy.

"There was Peggy Sue, a German short-haired pointer whose owners would play Buddy Holly on their stereo. The excitement we experienced when we heard her name is indescribable. We would immediately go to the door and whimper to be let out. How proudly we trotted under the gaudy scattering of stars! How immodest we were under the moon's opalescence! We pranced and pranced in the exuberant light."

"You make it sound so hunky-dory. There must've been bad times."

"The worst times were when my owners laughed. Suddenly they became strangers. The soft cadences of their conversation, the sharpness of their commands, gave way to howls, gurgles, and yelps. It was as if something were released in them, something absolute and demonic. Once they started it was hard for them to stop. You can't imagine how frightening and confusing it was to see my protectors out of control. The sounds they made seemed neither expressive or communicative, nor did they indicate pleasure or pain, but rather a weird mixture of both. It was a limbo of utterance from which I felt completely excluded. But why go on, those days are past."

"How do you know?"

"I just do. I feel it."

"But if you were a dog once, why not a dog twice?"

"Because there are no signs of that happening again. When I was a dog, there were indications that I would end up as I am now. I never liked exposing myself and was pained by having to perform private acts in public. I was embarrassed by the pomp of bitches in heat—their preening and wagging, by the panting lust of my brothers. I became withdrawn; I brooded; I actually suffered a kind of canine *terribilità*. It all pointed to one thing."

When Glover had finished, he waited for Tracy to speak. He was sorry he had told her so much. He felt ashamed. He hoped she would understand his having been a dog was not his choice, that such aberrations are born of necessity and are not lamentable. At times, the fury of a man's humanity will find its finest manifestation in amazing alterations of expectedness. For people are only marginally themselves. Glover, who earlier in the night had begun to slide into an agony of contrition, now felt righteous pride. He saw that Tracy's eyes were closed. She had fallen asleep. The truth had been endurable, had been overshadowed by a need that led her safely into the doom of another night. They would wake in the early morning and look at each other as always. What he had told her would be something they would never mention again, not out of politeness, or sensitivity for the other, but because such achievements of frailty, such lyrical lapses, are unavoidable in every life.

Two Stories

I

I T W A S A U T U M N I N C O N N E C T I C U T. I T
was breezy. The wind shook the trees, sending red and
yellow leaves spiraling to the ground, and made waves in
the small tan fields. The sky was clear. Its thin, darkening
blue was tinged with the yellow of afternoon. This was the
best possible light: everything shone. Rhodesia Brearley
stared from the dining room of her father's large colonial
house out to the stables. The light was perfect. She would
change into her breeches and boots and ride Victor, the
black gelding her father had given her on her birthday. She
imagined herself, serene and capable, cantering over the
fields of western Connecticut, all of autumn swirling
around her. In a mansion not far away, Golden Harris got
up from the desk in the study, where he was having tea,
and went to the living-room window. He stared at the

49

manicured lawn, which seemed almost blue. The moment
was ripe, he thought, for a spin in the Porsche. It was new,
a gift from his mother. He put on a blazer and walked
over the gravel drive to the garage. It was breezy. Red and
yellow leaves spun to the ground. The light was perfect; it
would make the crimson of his Porsche seem deeper and
darker. Rhodesia Brearley sat astride Victor. She had tied
a green ribbon in her auburn hair. She held the reins firmly
in her gloved hands. She led Victor over a low stone wall
into a field. The sky was still clear. Rhodesia was happy.
Love was not out of the question, she thought. A man
with rough hands and sweet breath would come, lift her
from Victor, and lead her into a barn that was clean and
quiet. Golden Harris leaned forward in the black leather
seat of the Porsche to turn the ignition key. The car
roared. Golden shifted it into reverse, then turned, shifted
again, and sped off over the gravel. The wind shook the
trees. The sky was a darkening blue. Golden headed for
Pine Ridge Road. He turned on his radio. Gluck's *Orfeo ed
Euridice* was on WNCN. Orfeo was singing, "Che puro
Ciel! Che chiaro sol!" How true, how true, said Golden to
himself. Rhodesia urged Victor on. She was happy and
wanted to sing. It didn't matter what. She wanted to toss
her voice into the air in an act of approval, of abandon.
She opened her mouth. She had no particular song in
mind. When the first note struck the air, Victor, as if
pierced by pain, stopped short and Rhodesia flew out of
the stirrups onto the ground. She was unhurt. But Victor
ran off, leaping stone walls and dashing through fields.
Golden was humming as Orfeo sang, "Che dolci lusin-
ghieri suoni . . ." A few leaves spun to the ground. The air
rushed by the car. Victor burst from the woods beside

e national anthem. But the general's
ugh to stop the enemy's advance. He
brooded while mortar fire rocked the
he air with bursts of blinding light.
his adjutant, who had been standing
I think we must do something dif-

the adjutant said.
and began to pace. "Something un-
and it may sound cruel, is that we
back into the fight, let them stagger
We must teach the foe a lesson."
ed pacing. He crinkled his brow and
t. "If that doesn't work, we'll send
out there nude—they'll dance across

a huge blast, and small bits of earth
own the sloping roof of the tent. The
Maybe dogs would work! We could

More men died. Perhaps from pity,
to conserve ammunition, the enemy
ment. But the periods of silence were

general was reading Clausewitz by
ughing could be heard. The general
it seemed to him that they were
on.
s of men coughing. No army that
he adjutant.
nt. The density of the night seemed
his sloping shoulders as the cares of

Pine Ridge Road at the instant Golden's Porsche appeared. The sky was deepening. The car shone in the
perfect light. Orfeo sang, ". . . al riposar eterno tutto
invita qui!" Victor tried to clear the Porsche in one magnificent leap, but crashed on the roof, his forelegs on
one side, his hind legs on the other. Stillness hung in the
autumn evening. The sky was deepening into red. Up
and down Pine Ridge Road, house lights were being
turned on.

I I

A beautiful woman stood at the roof-edge of one of New
York's tall midtown apartment houses. She was on the
verge of jumping when a man, coming out on the roof to
sunbathe, saw her. Surprised, the woman stepped back
from the ledge. The man was about thirty or thirty-five
and blond. He was lean, with a long upper body and short,
thin legs. His black bathing suit shone like satin in the sun.
He was no more than ten steps from the woman. She
stared at him. The wind blew strands of her long dark hair
across her face. She pulled them back and held them in
place with one hand. Her white blouse and pale blue skirt
kept billowing, but she paid no attention. He saw that she
was barefooted and that two high-heeled shoes were
placed side by side on the gravel near where she stood.
She had turned away from him. The wind flattened her
skirt against the front of her long thighs. He wished he
could reach out and pull her toward him. The air shifted
and drew her skirt tightly across her small, round buttocks; the lines of her bikini underpants showed. "I'll take

you to dinner," he yelled. The woman turned to look at him again. Her gaze was point-blank. Her teeth were clenched. The man looked at her hands which were now crossed in front of her, holding her skirt in place. She wore no wedding band. "Let's go someplace and talk," he said. She took a deep breath and turned away. She lifted her arms as if she were preparing to dive. "Look," he said, "if it's me you're worried about, you have nothing to fear." He took the towel he was carrying over his shoulders and made it into a sarong. "I know it's depressing," he said. He was not sure what he had meant. He wondered if the woman felt anything. He liked the way her back curved into her buttocks. It struck him as simple and expressive; it suggested an appetite or potential for sex. He wished he could touch her. As if to give him some hope, the woman lowered her arms to her sides and shifted her weight. "I'll tell you what," the man said, "I'll marry you." The wind once again pulled the woman's skirt tightly across her buttocks. "We'll do it immediately," he said, "and then go to Italy. We'll go to Bologna, we'll eat great food. We'll walk around all day and drink grappa at night. We'll observe the world and we'll read the books we never had time for." The woman had not turned around or backed off from the ledge. Beyond her lay the industrial buildings of Long Island City, the endless row houses of Queens. A few clouds moved in the distance. The man shut his eyes and tried to think of how else to change her mind. When he opened them, he saw that between her feet and the ledge was a space, a space that would always exist now between herself and the world. In the long moment when she existed before him for the last time, he thought, How lovely. Then she was gone.

flashes of gunfire, t
bravery was not en
sat in his tent and
ground and shook
Finally, he turned t
nearby, and said, "
ferent."

"What is that, sir?
The general got u
usual. What I mean
must get the wounde
unarmed into battle.

The general stopp
stared at the adjuta
some of our soldiers
no-man's-land."

Close by there was
pattered and rolled d
general continued, "
send a division."

Things got worse.
perhaps from a need
eased up its bombard
also frightening.

One night while th
candlelight, enemy co
cocked his head and
coughing in his directi

"Sir, those are tap
sick could fight," said

The general was sil
to weigh as heavily on

war. He slumped in his chair. He stroked his grizzled chin. "Suppose we made them believe they were sick! Suppose we parachuted in a few hundred nurses! Suppose we did it at night and the nurses wore uniforms that shone in the dark!"

A look of astonishment crossed the adjutant's face. "That's a beautiful idea, sir."

"Does it surprise you," responded the general, "that a military man like myself has a sweet tooth for beauty? That one of the finest military minds of our time worships Rembrandt and cries a lot?

"One more thing, adjutant. If you're captured, suck your thumb and whimper. The enemy will think you're a child or an idiot, and they won't harm you."

I I

PRESIDENT: Hi, Mel, is that you?

GENERAL: Yes, sir.

PRESIDENT: You sound far away.

GENERAL: I am, sir.

PRESIDENT: Listen, Mel, I like the job you did.

GENERAL: But we lost, and we didn't have to.

PRESIDENT: Yes we did, Mel. We did what we had to. We won by losing. Our humanity can never again be questioned. Just imagine what the world would think if we'd won, if we'd blasted those devils!

GENERAL: I got it, sir. But still, I feel that we should have won this one.

PRESIDENT: Oh, Mel, Mel, it's better this way. Weakness is strength. We're a complex people and nothing breeds fear like complexity. They're afraid of us, Mel, because they don't know what we'll do next.

GENERAL: Who's afraid, sir?

PRESIDENT: The whole rotten world, the whole snivelling mess of nations, everybody—every man, woman, and child!

III

A calm settled on the small country that had been torn to pieces by war. Birds glided overhead. Leaves flooded the high branches of trees. Small groups of chattering people walked in the streets only partly cleared of rubble. There was nothing much to do. Both sides were pulling out, both sides had made a point.

In a hotel near the capital, the general prepared to go home. With the adjutant standing by, holding a towel, the general stretched out in a tub of gray water, soaped himself, and splashed the waves.

"Oh the waves, I love the waves, the pearly waves, don't you, adjutant?"

"Yes, sir, I do."

"You know, adjutant, I was an unhappy and sickly child. Would you believe it, what with all this hair on my chest?"

"No, sir, I would not."

"Well then, adjutant, you'd be making a big mistake."

The adjutant smiled. The general was happy. The war was over. Soon they'd be home.

Later, the general and the adjutant were standing in the middle of a large dressing room, gazing into the full-length mirror of a mahogany armoire. The general was turning this way and that. The adjutant held a bottle of cologne, poised to spray.

"Do you think I'm good-looking?" the general asked.

"Yes, sir, I do."

"Am I better with or without my cap?"

"Without it, sir."

"What about my dress uniform, adjutant, does it look better on me than fatigues?"

"That's hard to say, sir."

"Hard, adjutant?"

"Yes, sir, hard."

"Are you saying it makes no difference?"

"No, sir."

The adjutant thought for a moment, then turning to the general he said, "Sir, I think you're a good-looking guy no matter what you wear."

I V

When the general entered his spartan suburban home, his wife April immediately put a trumpet to her lips and began to play Taps. She had the gift of putting him at ease.

They sat beside each other on the couch. He took her hand and kissed it, and he remembered her as she stood in front of the bears' cage that day in the zoo when they met. She was a small, neatly dressed woman with straight black hair that hung almost to her waist. But her most striking feature was her plump buttocks that arched out from the small of her back and perched proudly on her muscular thick legs. He remembered that his attention was torn between April and the bears. In their loose covering of fur, slowly shambling in the city's foul air, the bears moved back and forth, heavy and slumberous, from rock to rock. He liked them, and it seemed to him that April did, too. They met every day for two weeks, in the same place. Then Melville Monroe asked April Rodriguez to marry him, and she accepted.

The pleasures of being at home were short-lived. The general missed the routines of war and spent more and more time in his room, standing at attention for long periods. It was a kind of homage to the armed forces, a prayer offered to his superiors. He would give himself the command out loud and then snap to attention.

During one of these bouts of standing, April walked in. She saw immediately that Mel had a love of the army and a feel for his country that was rare. She stared at him, and something in his eyes—something wistful, something secret, something that evoked distance and darkness, savvy and sweetness—excited her. No one had to tell her what to do. She stood with her man, at attention.

V

PRESIDENT: Hi, Mel, is that you?

GENERAL: Yes, sir.

PRESIDENT: You sound far away.

GENERAL: I am, sir.

PRESIDENT: Listen, Mel, I like the job you did, and I want you to do another.

GENERAL: What's that, sir?

PRESIDENT: In order to reemphasize our humanity, Mel, we're

going to defend the right of a small country to rule itself. We're going back to war.

GENERAL: Very good, sir.

PRESIDENT: And, Mel, no rough stuff. Kill a few men, but lay off the women and kids. Thanks, Mel, I know you'll do a good job.

V I

The new war went the way of the previous one. The general was losing and had ceased to care. What did it matter? What did anything matter? The general now saw the vanity of things—the pomp that elevates the everyday and embellishes emptiness. He saw how childish and boastful was the military's practice of wearing medals and ribbons, of making grown men sport their dossiers on their chests. So what if the army gave him a comfortable pension and relieved him of any further need to wage limited wars of peace. There was no reason for him to remain in the service. He had nothing to guide him from moment to moment—no desire, no purpose. His days were long and lustreless, and April was far away, and the adjutant could not be expected to share an old warrior's disillusionment. Let the trumpets blare for others, let parades go on without him.

The general, with his head high, walked unarmed to the minefield. When he got there, he ran around, trying to step on a mine. Once in a while a flare would show him in the pursuit of death—scampering, whirling, jumping like a bunny. It did not work. He survived, crawled into a bush on the enemy side, disguised his voice, and taunted his men into firing at him. They kept missing. He went to where the enemy tanks were rolling, and lay on the ground, waiting to be run over. But the rolling, churning tanks went off in another direction. Death would not have him, would not even come close.

VII

The general went home a changed man. Lost in the calm of civilian life, he tried to impose on himself a set of rituals that would order his day. He was not successful. Golf, gardening, looking at real estate, nothing could hold his attention. Even April seemed dull. For a while, he hoped the President would call, but he never did. Nor did the adjutant ever visit for old time's sake. The general missed the excitement of wartime. He longed to hear the angelic thunder of distant guns, the soft drumming and shuffle of troops on parade. He lived with a sense of war's majestic purpose, its patterns of doom, its grave delights. He sat in his rocker, reliving the old campaigns and thinking of ways they might have been won. More and more time was spent in blissful revision. He bought hundreds of toy soldiers and deployed them on the porch. Their numbers swelled into the thousands. They took over the ground floor of the house while the general hovered above them like a doting Mars. His army won battles, again and again outsmarting the enemy. Tanks and armored vehicles lay overturned in the carpet's battered shag, dead troops were strewn from wall to wall. The general's gift for winning was great. He and April spent hours listening to tapes of the sounds of war, the whistling fall of bombs, the crack of rifles, the cries of men in combat.

Even now, the battles continue. Late at night, when the neighborhood sleeps, you can hear the fury of aerial bombardment, the bombs bursting in air, the marching men, the bugle calls, and above all, the general's voice rising into the sorrowful dark, giving orders.

Mr. and Mrs. Baby

MR. AND MRS. BABY
WAKE UP

I T IS MORNING IN CALIFORNIA. THE
sea, parading its troughs, flashing its foamy crests, keeps
heaving itself onto the shore. And the sky sends a delicate spread of caressing light, to discover the place where
the Babys lie buried in the sheeted, blanketed world of
slumber. How peaceful they seem. How lucky they are
that the difference between sleep and wakefulness can be
blurred, diminished, and finally erased without pain. Their
waking is a slow rising from crumpled linen and its odors
of cologne into lazy, tentative gestures of lovemaking. Yet
in an hour's time how close to sadness they will be in the
world of light, its ordeals of fixity, of ornament, of re-
sponsibility: Baby Hades.

HOW MR. AND MRS. BABY
LOOKED

Mr. and Mrs. Baby looked familiar. Bob Baby had the wide but serious mouth of Alan Roscoe when he played in *The Last of the Mohicans,* and his blue eyes were like Bing Crosby's in *The Bells of St. Mary's,* with the same soft, other-worldly look; yet at times they took on the stern, no-nonsense gaze that was Bing's in *Going My Way.* His black hair fell down over his right eye the way Gable's always did. His cheeks had the fallen firmness of Ronald Colman's in *Lost Horizon* or Richard Egan's in *Khyber Patrol.* But the marvellous jaw was straight Cooper—the Cooper of *Beau Geste.* His nose was Heston's, with the same tip and the same slant of nostril. His walk and his air of purpose were just a cut below Kenneth More's in *The Admirable Crichton*—he always dreamed of going tux-edoed to the beach. His ears were unmistakably Herbert Marshall's, and his eyebrows were perfectly peaked, with just the right amount of hair; in other words, they were Errol Flynn's—the great Flynn of *The Charge of the Light Brigade.* His body, alas, was undistinguished, with the same bleached rubescence of Walter Slezak's in all his movies since *Once Upon a Honeymoon.*

Babe Baby's face had the transcendental sweetness of Laura La Plante's. But her eyes had the softness, the downward slant of Vilma Banky's in *Son of the Sheik.* And yet there was a touch, especially in her left eye, of Dolores Costello. Her cheeks were high but several notches lower than Garbo's, and they had the fullness of Claudette Colbert's, especially when she smiled. Babe had

a wholesomeness, too, that was given its imprimatur by
her nose. It was not perfectly shaped like Gloria Gra-
hame's, not barren like Betty Hutton's, not swaybacked
like Ingrid Bergman's, nor with oversized nostrils like
Donna Reed's or Joan Bennett's; it was a nose like the
radiant Janet Blair's. It was perky without being prying, it
was cute without being cheap, it was noble without being
undemocratic. Babe wore her light brown hair swept back
and short, the way Norma Shearer did in *A Free Soul*. Her
walk was pure assurance, pure Lauren Bacall. And she
was as poised, when occasion dictated, as Celeste Holm in
Gentleman's Agreement or Lilli Palmer in *The Counterfeit
Traitor*. Best of all, she had the robust aquatic self-
possession of Esther Williams in *Pagan Love Song*.

MR. AND MRS. BABY
AT BREAKFAST

The ease they felt in each other's presence, though
tinged at times with regret, even unhappiness—deep unhappiness, even; irreversible misery, it could be said—
allowed them to share some of what was on their minds.
And like so many who have spent years together, they
could anticipate each other's questions as well as answers.
Thus, at breakfast, Bob knew what Babe was thinking
when he said, "So you want to know where they came
from. And you want to know how they came. They came
from Poland and Russia, from France and Germany, from
Turkey and the Congo, from Iceland and Italy; they came
from China and the Philippines; they came and they came,
and they brought their aunts and cousins, sisters and
brothers, mothers and fathers; they brought them by boat,

by train, by plane; they walked and they ran and they came with satchels, trunks, suitcases, boxes; they kept coming in waves, in droves, in trickles, but they kept coming; they came at night or in bright day; they came in the wrecking storm, they came in the calm of noon; they came waving their arms, stamping their feet, speaking Dutch, Rumanian, Serbian, Czech, Urdu; they came with hats or without—it made no difference to those hearty people; they wore dark suits and long dresses; many were overweight, but they came and they came. Some were professors, some were bricklayers, some were chicken farmers, but they came, and they went to Arizona and Iowa and Illinois; they came and they went to Nebraska and Alabama and Maryland; they came and they went to Pennsylvania, Montana, and Hawaii. They were the Smiths, the Goldbergs, the Rodriguezes, the Babys. Yes, the Babys were part of it, were half of it, were all of it. Everyone was a Baby and the Babys were everyone."

Babe was silent, then slowly began to laugh in nervous acknowledgment of the vistas that opened before her, and behind her in case she unexpectedly turned around. Out of control, her laughter increased in tempo. She shook and snorted, and even howled, in tribute to what she had heard. Bob, taken with the unexpected sweep of his speech, could not have been more pleased by her response.

MRS. BABY HAS
AN EXPERIENCE

Babe pulled herself together and went to the beach, some books of poetry tucked under her arm. She thought more about the future than she did of the past. And she believed the daily unfolding of events was oblivious of her needs. What were her needs? And who needed them anyway? She sat on the sand, read a little, then drifted into thought.

How did I get here if not below the surface, allowing the deep you-know-what to figure things out? How did I get here, if not in Bob's blue Mercedes disappearing down into the canyon, then into this vanishing light? Fix your eyes on the sea and its lunging; lounge, as you will, in semi-coma, remembering the hand trucks of opportunity, the boatloads of promise that were exchanged for this distant now, its plungings, its watery walls, its towers of bubble! Lie back and be stirred by the glitter of sense, as if you were the maker of the words you heard, heard almost as medleyed sound, a maker of the words you might utter; for you are the maker of the words you heard, and if there is another maker he is nowhere near.

This sudden rush of thoughts scared Babe, scored itself deep into her vision of self—scarred her, in fact—so she decided to say nothing to Bob of the mysterious turn her mind had taken.

MR. BABY ALSO HAS
AN EXPERIENCE

There is a time of day when quietness invades the landscape and takes up residence in all the things one sees. Every leaf, every cloud is suddenly still and is viewed with unusual clarity, and in that moment it is as if the destiny of each thing were revealed. This awesome ascent into consciousness, into luminous, crystalline recognition was not lost on Mr. Baby, who stood alone on the lawn in front of his house. Brought outside by a restlessness whose source was obscure, he was likewise brought out of himself into a spacious aura of epiphanous light, into an openness of being that took him by surprise. With a knowledge almost too deep for tears, he saw all things ablaze with the glory of their own mortality. He lingered until the world around him suddenly resumed its normal aspect, then he went inside and began to pace on the green living-room rug. He wondered why he was here and not there, why he had chosen the life he had instead of the life he hadn't, why he felt as he did and, sometimes, as he didn't. Thus it was that Bob Baby wrote his first poem and decided to say nothing about it to Babe.

MR. AND MRS. BABY
SKIP LUNCH

At making do or doing without, the Babys wished to think themselves accomplished. So at lunch, when neither of them took the time to sit down and have a bite, it was done with a grace bordering on the regal. They felt the glory of self-abnegation because they understood too well the degradation of fulfillment. There would be no linen tablecloth today, no silverware, no succession of dishes each with its own bouquet of steam which seemed to ripen in the hazy sunlit air of the dining room. There would be no *tonnarelli alla ciociara,* those thin linguine-like noodles in a sauce of fresh *funghi,* no light, smoky Gavi dei Gavi to wash it down with, or even a *pasticcio con melanzane* so reminiscent of Sicily; no *mozzarella in carrozza,* no beef tongue with green sauce, no grilled zucchini with Sardo cheese, no *pissaladière provençale* with its hefty aroma of anchovy and onion, no *clafouti* of Bing cherries touched with ginger. There would be no bare table and paper napkins even, no sandwiches, odorless and sterile in small dishes, no gaunt glasses of apple juice, no stopgap noshes of any sort. The dining room would be empty, and the Babys would bask in the image of its foodless clarity and silently applaud the splendor of its austerity, the clean denial of its destiny.

MR. AND MRS. BABY
HAVE A GOOD CRY

It was as if the exertion of denial had proved too much, and the ache of emptiness had become more than a meal put aside. They sank into listlessness, each of them slumped in a chair, staring outside, emitting weak, barely audible sighs. The restorative power of consciousness that had worked its magic on them only hours before was now lacking. Each of them felt defeated by a motif that missing lunch was only the most obvious sign of. They were not speaking. It was as if they had forgotten how. They were estranged even from each other. It was this, perhaps, that made them seem now smaller and more frail than ever, and why their sighs gave way to tears and sniffles. They looked at each other pathetically, their eyes seeming to ask: Why, why do we feel this way? The answer came with a volley of sobs and a downpour of tears. The Babys wept without shame.

MR. AND MRS. BABY
HAVE A TALK

Bob and Babe dried their eyes and looked at each other with an intensity that had been lacking in the moments preceding their cry. And the way each of them sat—Babe with her legs crossed, Bob with his hands clasped behind his head—seemed to suggest that life was good.

"Life *is* good," said Babe. "It's crazy for us to feel the way we did."

"Say," said Bob. "How about we have a bite?"

"Do you think we should?" said Babe. "Don't you think that'd be gilding the lily? I mean, we don't have to eat just to prove life is good."

"I know what you mean," said Bob. Conscious of how much they had been through, he felt mellow. The stillness of the room, its warm, sunlit air, contributed to a feeling of having arrived. Everything seemed balanced, complete. It was easy to give in to the benevolence of fate; life was not only good, it was worth waiting for.

"We are such fools," said Babe.

Somewhere up the street a dog barked, and gave up, and barked again. The sound was forlorn and seemed to measure the silence instead of breaking it. Bob didn't mind. He liked the way the afternoon was winding down, the gradual lengthening of shadows everywhere. A small breeze entered the room, barely shaking the sheer muslin curtains. "I know what you mean," he said.

"I'm so happy at this moment I could cry," said Babe, and she jumped up, went quickly to Bob, and kissed him lightly on the cheek. Bob smiled, his hands clasped behind his head.

MR. AND MRS. BABY
GO TO A PARTY

Sometimes on summer evenings, when the light is almost gone, when everything has taken on a heavy, exhausted aspect, there can be felt in the air a restlessness, a furtive rustling, a burgeoning of desire. This evening, while the Babys prepared to go out, the urgency of promised adventure was so palpable that the neighborhood seemed to murmur with pleasure. And when they walked to the party, they were almost overcome with the magical intimacy of leaves saturating the air with the odor of green, the sweet seasoning of summer. Furtive above them, above the motionless canopy of maples, was the open gaze of the moon.

Everyone at the party, drifters and flitters, merged willingly into the amiable flow. Round and round they went with round after round of drink, their voices, muted by the low-ceilinged interior, mingling naturally with the barely audible sounds coming from the stereo. There was no change all evening.

Nothing was happening. The Babys stayed only as long as they had to and then walked home.

MR. AND MRS. BABY
GO TO SLEEP

Now, at day's end, the Babys slip naked into bed, their limbs overcome with weariness, their minds dimming, giving way to the power and grandeur of nothingness, the silent ohs and ahs of oblivion. Oh Babys! Ah Babys! Whither now? Whither later? It's all the same. Among the celestial acts in the theatre of night, in the superdome of the firmament, where distance is a monotonous allegory of diminishment, a shifting of solar dust, a waltzing of matter to the tune of darkness, a grave passage of this and that, what does it mean that you are asleep, adrift in the spectral silt of the unknown? What has the relentless fury of particles to do with you? Pull your covers up to your chins. Sleep tight; another Baby day is on its way.

Wooley

I SPEAK OF GEORGE WOOLEY, MY FRIEND
Wooley the watchful. Wooley the wily. Wooley the warm.
I speak of him because he is dead. The world never knew
him, never gave him a chance, and he passed unacknowl-
edged into his grave.

Wooley was a dashing figure—a sportsman, an inventor
of games, a poet, a tireless lover. He moved with the ease
of the famous—as if a red carpet were unrolling perpetually before him. He wore tailored tweed jackets, faded
cotton shirts, Italian corduroy pants, Justin boots. His
wavy hair, which he combed straight back, was sandy-
colored and matched his eyes. Women adored him, but
not for long. He always moved on. He was Wooley the
wild to some. Wooley the weird to others. To me he was
Wooley the wonder.

It is the shadow of Wooley's voice that you hear in mine. I was nothing until I met Wooley; I remember his words when he described his Rocky Mountain retreat to some dinner guests one night. He looked up to the ceiling. His hands were before him as if he were holding an invisible basketball. And he began: "There you would see cloud towers, floating bushes of shade, great scoops of vapor, milky mountains of air, blouses blown up and away, buttocks adrift, bleached wigs, powdery potatoes, albino clods, blurred faces of everybody you ever knew, all the paraphernalia of sleep—eiderdowns, pillows, and nimble sheep—strung along high winds, hissing their long, unfinished histories, passing from east to west day after day, with monotonous comic appeal and mysterious pomp, over hot, haze-filled cities. . . ." I tell you he was out of sight! When he finished, there was silence except for me, his old friend, who began to weep. It was not only the beauty of his speech but the odor of Gorgonzola sauce rising from the gnocchi on my plate that undid me. Unparalleled, heavenly incongruity!

Compared with Wooley's, the lives of all my other friends seemed aimless. They complained of boredom. An excess of afternoons, Wooley would have said. Tom and Harriet, Pete and Greeny, Phil, Floss, Willis, Milly—the whole gang, they never understood him. They were shocked when he challenged Monty Bianco, the tennis star, to a match at the field club. They were concerned when an ambulance pulled up at courtside and a heavily bandaged, wobbling Wooley was helped to the court, with racquet in hand. When Monty saw him, his eyes bulged in disbelief. He didn't know what to do until Wooley, his voice cracking with anguish, told him to serve. Monty served three double faults. On the fourth point Wooley returned Monty's first service but released a scream of such hideous magnitude that if an elephant with a human voice had watched its children slaughtered it would not have sounded as pained. Monty was stunned and missed his shot. At this moment the hired ambulance driver and attendant rushed out to help the brave Wooley back into the ambulance. What a breath of fresh air his humor was!

Wooley was a fabulous inventor of games, but they were often misunderstood. Death, his greatest, was probably ahead of its time. It was played on a Monopoly-like board, and each player picked at random a card telling him what disease he would have for the duration of the game. The object was to avert death as long as possible, and the winner was the one who outlived the others. Wooley, why did you have to die!

He loved children. But the dolls he invented for them could never be marketed. They came in little sickbeds or in wheelchairs, and, reversing the usual fate of dolls, were programmed to get well or to walk again if given love and encouragement. Some would reward the child with heart-felt utterances like "I can walk! I can walk!" or, "I can see! I can see!" Oh, shortsighted parents! If only you had known him!

I remember asking him about the days when he was in love with Isabel Bell and his saying, "That was another season of the year—a vague indefinable season, whose trees were neither with leaves nor without, whose air was neither warm nor cold. I have no memory of the days or of the time." Not a mean word about Isabel, who left him for the flashy Monty Bianco. How considerate, how selfless.

When I asked him how he felt after his father cut him off without a penny, he said, "I would go out under the stars and enter the smallness of being that was mine, and I would disappear into the emptiness within, and it seemed enormous." Again there was no anger.

Once, while we were swimming, I asked him if things came easily to him. He said, "I see the world through a small eye, an eye so small the world does not notice." I was so moved by his answer I almost drowned.

But it was Wooley who drowned, a few years later, while skating with Milly and Pete and Greeny and Floss and me. We were out on the lake at night, standing around a fire, smoking cigarettes, listening to Wooley tell us about the dark towns of central Europe, each with its own muddy main street over which chickens strutted aimlessly. Suddenly he skated away over the endless black pane of ice. None of us followed him. Under the stillness of the night sky, we stood together, a shivering, frightened little group, and through the cold dark flew the sound of our voices calling, "Wooley, Wooley, Wooley!"

Zadar

THERE ARE TIMES WHEN TO BE ALONE is to be seized with panic. It happens usually in places far from home where the language is unknown, where one is without friends, and where none of the props by which emptiness is concealed or disguised are at hand. Distraction is impossible. It is a panic that even seasoned travellers are familiar with. In the face of it, the most ephemeral smile, a drink warming in the sun, the sudden shade of a small cloud, achieve a false significance. It is in this avoidance of self that we become sentimental.

The last trip I had taken was to Zadar on the Dalmatian coast. I stayed at the Hotel Zagreb, a big nineteenth-century building with a café that looks out on a narrow channel of bright water and a long, low, sparsely wooded island. I was sitting alone, having a Campari, nervously turning the glass, feeling at loose ends and wondering whether I should leave Zadar, when I saw a woman of such sullen beauty that for the moment I banished any thought of escaping. She sat at the next table, leaning on her elbows and, from time to time, passing the back of her hand, in an upward sweeping gesture, between the nape of her neck and her dishevelled golden hair. She was with a man who stared across the channel to the island. Despite the heat, they had not touched their drinks. Their silence made me think they were very much at ease with each other, that neither of them felt they had to awaken in the other displays of passion by which their feelings could be declared and, consequently, measured. Theirs was probably a friendship (neither wore a wedding band) without pain and without profundity. Perhaps it was their dislike of being alone more than their desire for each other that drew them together. Did they speak as lovers—sketching in their lives before they met, shedding small light on the mysteries of their pasts? I figured their relationship depended on a hard, comfortless exclusivity. When they rose to leave, I was struck by the woman's shoulders, which were drawn slightly forward, and by her long calves and thin ankles. When I looked up to see her face, which despite its sensuality seemed taut even to the point of severity, she was staring at me. Then she turned and left with the man.

Later, after the sun had set, I walked to the center of town. The image of the woman was inescapable. I began to think there was something accusatory in her stare, something defeated in the way she carried her shoulders. Then I thought of her legs; I stood before the facade of the church of St. Mary with its round Venetian gables rising wearily into the summer darkness and imagined the woman lifting her skirt slowly, showing me her thighs—their thinness, their smoothness—touched by light. The sound of her skirt brushing against them sent a shiver down my spine. Then as if a prayer had been answered, when I turned from the church, I saw her walking in front of an outdoor café, heading toward the hotel. She was wearing a pale green, tight-fitting dress that exaggerated the curves of her body. From the crook of her arm swung a white purse. Walking a few steps behind was the man. I followed them to the hotel and waited outside to see, when they turned on their lights, which room was theirs.

The next morning I had my coffee at a table in front of the hotel where I could look up at their window. But the woman never appeared, and I finally walked to where a rowboat waited that would ferry me across the harbor. It was a bright day and when the rowboat deposited me at the breakwater in Borik, I set off for the beach. I walked down avenues flanked with decaying nineteenth-century mansions, large summer homes, shuttered and gray, and barren open lots where the poured-concrete shells of unfinished houses seemed already abandoned by their owners. At the beach I rented a boat and rowed, then drifted and read the novel I brought with me. I took off my shirt and the sun warmed my back and shoulders. I found it hard to concentrate. Every once in a while a voice carried over the water, and I would look up to see if I could spot whose it was. To my astonishment, at the back of the beach, standing in their street clothes was the couple. They looked as if they were arguing. My heartbeat quickened as I considered the possibility of his leaving her or of my coming to her rescue. Suddenly, he turned and walked away. She stood where she was, then looked to the water where she saw me in the boat, staring at her. She smiled, then reached up under her skirt, pulled down her panties, and put them in her purse. The swift, unexpected vulgarity of her gesture so shook me that I almost fell out of the boat.

In the late afternoon, the café in front of the Zagreb fills with people who have come to watch the sunset in the first cool breeze of evening. Everyone gathers in the faintly aromatic air of dusk while above them the leaves of trees form a tattered canopy and the thin trunks blacken. A foreigner, like myself, who had no idea of what is being said around him, can watch the boats move back and forth on the dark waters of the channel. The woman's chin rested on her folded hands and she continued to look away from the man. He was silent. There was a slight tear in her dress near the left shoulder and another in the sleeve just above her left elbow. She seemed calm; her mouth was relaxed and her gray-green eyes were touched with what I took to be longing. I wondered whether the tears in her dress were the results of a struggle, whether their arguments came to actual blows, and if she ever retaliated physically. I considered the possible violence of their lovemaking. And my gaze drifted out to the small boats moving in the channel.

I neither blamed nor forgave myself for behavior that was clearly at odds with my nature. My sudden obsession was so great and so pleasurable that the intrusion of conscience, besides causing unhappiness and self-chastisement, would have cleared the way for the very panic I dreaded. I lingered outside the hotel and continued to ponder what sort of relationship the couple had. The woman might be unhappy because of something she did that could not be undone, something that had hurt the man she was with. Perhaps her silence was the result of a bitter refusal to accept blame or feel guilt for having had an affair. On the other hand, the way she avoided looking at him might be simple resignation, might even be boredom.

Again I had my breakfast where I could keep an eye on their window. When she appeared in a thin, white bathrobe to look out over the water, I could make out the hazy outline of her body. When she turned to go back into the room, her bathrobe opened and I saw a blur of flesh. Again, she must have known I was watching because in a moment she returned and stood with her bathrobe open, just as before. I stared up at the window as if stricken. How long it lasted I can't say. Even later, as I looked at the tall Byzantine church of St. Donat and walked in Nazor Park, I considered whether I should go to her hotel room. I kept seeing her vague flesh behind the wash of window and kept thinking that she lay in bed, waiting for me.

Later that day it had grown overcast, threatening rain, and a wind ruffled the awnings of the cafés. On the streets there were few people. Out on the water, the small boats bobbed, their bells clanking. I went to the museum, where I wandered from room to room, peering into glass cases filled with gold and silver reliquaries. I was too restless to really see anything and I was also troubled by a slight foreboding. So when I entered the last room, I was not entirely surprised to discover the woman standing there as if she expected me. I have often felt that behind the world we choose for ourselves there is another, unchosen, unaccounted for, that chooses us. It is the world of accidents, of chance encounters, and wishes fulfilled. Only rarely does it allow itself to be seen and when it does it claims us totally. Usually, it terrifies or thrills us and we are lifted far from the safety of our normal round of choices. Which is why, at that moment, it never occurred to me that I didn't know what to do or say. I walked over to the woman and took her hand.

Outside in the dusk, a few large drops of rain had fallen. We were hurrying to the hotel. It had not crossed my mind until that moment to speak, and it wasn't fear of banality that kept me silent, nor was it because I suspected that we had no language in common, it was because she was leading me and I had no intention of stopping her. Why should I ask, Where are we going?, when it was becoming obvious, or ask, Suppose that man I've seen you with is there?, when it seemed to me that she didn't care and didn't think I should either.

When we were in the tiny hotel elevator, she took my hand and drew it around her waist and I leaned down and kissed her. I kissed her again just as the elevator door was opening and once again, very briefly, when we stopped in front of the door to her room. She took the key from her purse but before she put it in the slot, she knocked. There was no response, so she went ahead and unlocked the door and we went in. I can still recall something of the weight of that day—its heavy overcast, its damp—and something very different, but just as tangible, to do with my sudden fear of the woman as I crossed the threshold. And in my memory something of the room's dark is mingled with the faint musk and jasmine odor of perfume, and there was, I recall, a red flower on the small table at the foot of the bed. I have often tried to gather around me the details of the moment I entered that room, but it was too shadowy and dark, and the streetlamp on the corner shed no more than a dim glow in the vicinity of the window. Uncertain of what to do, I stood by the door, watching her as she stood in the almost-dark by the bed and slowly, very slowly, almost languorously, undressed. I felt lost, bewildered by what was happening, and my desire seemed borrowed and remote. Then she came over to me and the strangeness suddenly passed. Outside, it had begun to rain very hard and I imagined the small boats tugging at their moorings.

It was close in the room. I think she would have opened the window but was afraid the rain would come in. I remember how cool her skin seemed as we lay on the bedspread and how quiet she was as the rain pattered against the glass; she hardly seemed to breathe. Then a flash of lightning lit up the whole room. And in the still-ness of that instant I felt small, incalculably so, and every-thing that was mine ceased to exist. I was in another world, one that seemed abandoned, thrust out of time, for seated in an easy chair, at the back of the room, was the man. He was staring at the bed. He wore a white shirt open at the neck and rolled up at the arms. I was afraid, afraid he would do something. But he didn't. In the not-so-secret dark I remained beside the woman and every so often I would run a finger slowly along her thigh or turn ever so slightly and brush my cheek against her shoulder. And soon I was no longer afraid. The man stared at the two of us, and the only sound he made was when he crossed and uncrossed his legs. He just stared and the woman lay beside me and I did nothing until it got light and then I left.

flashes of gunfire, the national anthem. But the general's bravery was not enough to stop the enemy's advance. He sat in his tent and brooded while mortar fire rocked the ground and shook the air with bursts of blinding light. Finally, he turned to his adjutant, who had been standing nearby, and said, "I think we must do something different."

"What is that, sir?" the adjutant said.

The general got up and began to pace. "Something unusual. What I mean, and it may sound cruel, is that we must get the wounded back into the fight, let them stagger unarmed into battle. We must teach the foe a lesson."

The general stopped pacing. He crinkled his brow and stared at the adjutant. "If that doesn't work, we'll send some of our soldiers out there nude—they'll dance across no-man's-land."

Close by there was a huge blast, and small bits of earth pattered and rolled down the sloping roof of the tent. The general continued, "Maybe dogs would work! We could send a division."

Things got worse. More men died. Perhaps from pity, perhaps from a need to conserve ammunition, the enemy eased up its bombardment. But the periods of silence were also frightening.

One night while the general was reading Clausewitz by candlelight, enemy coughing could be heard. The general cocked his head and it seemed to him that they were coughing in his direction.

"Sir, those are tapes of men coughing. No army that sick could fight," said the adjutant.

The general was silent. The density of the night seemed to weigh as heavily on his sloping shoulders as the cares of

The General

I

THE BATTLEFIELD HAD BEEN QUIET all morning. The twisted wrecks of armored equipment lay on the barren, cratered plain. Clouds of dust swirled around the charred debris.

General Melville Monroe worried about the morale of his troops. Their faces worn by fatigue, their uniforms reeking of sweat, they lay at his feet, dozing or puffing on cigarettes. Every so often, one of the men would sob or scream. Something had to be done. It was up to the general to prove that the war was worth fighting. Rather than make a speech, he walked to the front and stood, shaking his fist at the enemy. "Go ahead, shoot, I dare you!" he yelled. Then he turned and walked back to the trenches with a stride like a bullfighter's. At night, under a yellowish moon, he returned and sang, among the streaks and you to dinner," he yelled. The woman turned to look at him again. Her gaze was point-blank. Her teeth were clenched. The man looked at her hands which were now crossed in front of her, holding her skirt in place. She wore no wedding band. "Let's go someplace and talk," he said. She took a deep breath and turned away. She lifted her arms as if she were preparing to dive. "Look," he said, "if it's me you're worried about, you have nothing to fear." He took the towel he was carrying over his shoulders and made it into a sarong. "I know it's depressing," he said. He was not sure what he had meant. He wondered if the woman felt anything. He liked the way her back curved into her buttocks. It struck him as simple and expressive; it suggested an appetite or potential for sex. He wished he could touch her. As if to give him some hope, the woman lowered her arms to her sides and shifted her weight. "I'll tell you what," the man said, "I'll marry you." The wind once again pulled the woman's skirt tightly across her buttocks. "We'll do it immediately," he said, "and then go to Italy. We'll go to Bologna, we'll eat great food. We'll walk around all day and drink grappa at night. We'll observe the world and we'll read the books we never had time for." The woman had not turned around or backed off from the ledge. Beyond her lay the industrial buildings of Long Island City, the endless row houses of Queens. A few clouds moved in the distance. The man shut his eyes and tried to think of how else to change her mind. When he opened them, he saw that between her feet and the ledge was a space, a space that would always exist now between herself and the world. In the long moment when she existed before him for the last time, he thought, How lovely. Then she was gone.

Pine Ridge Road at the instant Golden's Porsche appeared. The sky was deepening. The car shone in the perfect light. Orfeo sang, ". . . al riposar eterno tutto invita qui!" Victor tried to clear the Porsche in one magnificent leap, but crashed on the roof, his forelegs on one side, his hind legs on the other. Stillness hung in the autumn evening. The sky was deepening into red. Up and down Pine Ridge Road, house lights were being turned on.

II

A beautiful woman stood at the roof-edge of one of New York's tall midtown apartment houses. She was on the verge of jumping when a man, coming out on the roof to sunbathe, saw her. Surprised, the woman stepped back from the ledge. The man was about thirty or thirty-five and blond. He was lean, with a long upper body and short, thin legs. His black bathing suit shone like satin in the sun. He was no more than ten steps from the woman. She stared at him. The wind blew strands of her long dark hair across her face. She pulled them back and held them in place with one hand. Her white blouse and pale blue skirt kept billowing, but she paid no attention. He saw that she was barefooted and that two high-heeled shoes were placed side by side on the gravel near where she stood. She had turned away from him. The wind flattened her skirt against the front of her long thighs. He wished he could reach out and pull her toward him. The air shifted and drew her skirt tightly across her small, round buttocks; the lines of her bikini underpants showed. "I'll take

Cephalus

CEPHALUS & PROCRIS

Procris was more beautiful than her sister Orithea, more beautiful than her famous actress mother. Something flowed in her that was different. She moved with a grace that seemed improvisational, athletic, animal. Yet there was nothing vulgar or provocative about her. When you spoke to her, she looked straight at you, her moist green eyes seeming to demand the truth. She paid strict attention to her experience, which made her wise beyond her years. And her seriousness translated itself into a powerful eroticism. This more than anything drew me to her.

The first months of our marriage were happy ones. We hung around the house, cooking, staring into the fire, and sleeping late. But after a while I began to feel the urge to go hunting again, and early one morning, while Procris slept, I got up and left the house, instinctively heading

toward a place where I remembered the hunting was good.
The sun was rising. It was getting warm. Before long I
stopped in a small clearing to take off my jacket. It was
suddenly very quiet, unnaturally so, and I knew I was
being watched. Then something moved in a nearby patch
of flowers. When I went to see what it was, I discovered a
naked woman sitting on a rock. She made no effort to
cover herself. Her calm, her cold features, her air of authority, made her appear aristocratic. "Who are you?" I
asked. "I'm Aurora," she said, and then walked up and
shook my hand. "I'm the goddess of dawn," she continued. "I see," I said, but all I really saw was her long legs,
her pubic hair, her breasts, her face that made me think of
Rita Hayworth except that her gaze had remarkable
power. Before I knew it she was leading me by the hand to
her cabin in the woods and I was on her bed and she was
leaning over me. "Please," I cried, "I love my wife."
"Shhh! Don't talk now," said Aurora as she nibbled at my
ear. "But it's true, I'm in love with Procris." "Shhh!" said
Aurora, and she put her hand gently over my mouth. My
resistance weakened until I finally yielded to her superior
strength. Afterwards, when we were having a drink, I
brought up the subject of leaving. But Aurora, who lay
back on a couple of pillows, still with no clothing on,
playing her fingertips lightly against her nipples, said, "I
want you to stay." And again, before I knew it, she was
unbuttoning my shirt and yanking off my pants. "It's
dark," she said, "you'd never find your way back." So I
spent the night. And I spent the next night, and the night
after that. It wasn't until the fourth day that I got something to eat and was allowed to put on my clothes. "I'm
worried about my wife," I said. "God knows what she

thinks happened to me." Aurora, tired of my complaints, said, "Well then, go back to her! But I'll tell you one thing, it won't do any good. I know a lot about the future and I know that marriages don't last. You'll come to wish you'd never met Procris." She sent me home without even a kiss goodbye.

On the way I did some thinking about what Aurora told me, and I began to worry. Had Procris slept with anyone while I was gone? Her youth and beauty suggested that someone would easily want to take advantage of her, but her character suggested the impossibility of that happening. Still, I'd been away for almost a week with no explanation. To expect her to be absolutely faithful in the light of my inexplicable absence might be asking too much. My own behavior was troublesome but especially in what it allowed me to imagine as a possibility for her. I was overcome with doubt and decided—lovers are foolish —to give myself a reason to have a grievance. I would put Procris' honor to the test. I changed my looks, got new clothes, and entered our town unrecognized.

When I got to the house, it looked the same, nothing I saw made me suspicious that anything unusual had gone on in my absence. I knocked at the door and Procris answered. The minute I saw her, I wanted to give up my ridiculous test and embrace her. I could tell she longed for her husband. The whites of her green eyes were touched with pink either from weeping or sleeplessness, her dark hair was loose and not drawn back from her face as it usually was, her lips were pale, and still she was beautiful. I told her I was a friend of her Cephalus. She said he was not at home, but invited me in anyway, hoping to hear some news of his whereabouts. It did her good to talk about him, for in the course of conversation she even smiled once or twice. When I returned the next day, with the express purpose of trying to figure out where her husband might be, she again smiled a little. But I must say that her look throughout each of the meetings was for the most part overwhelmingly earnest, even glum. I tried to comfort her with a little jollity. "Well, if Cephalus doesn't return, you can always marry me. I'd never leave your side." "I don't care how long it takes," she replied, "I'm waiting for him." And she showed me out. The next day it was hard to reach her. Finally, when I got hold of her, she consented to talk to me only because I told her I had news of Cephalus. "He was spotted by a friend of mine in the city," I said. And then I invited her out, saying that Cephalus would not mind, after all he and I were old friends. She declined, saying, "I don't know what you have in mind, but I want it known that I'm not going out with anyone." What more could any rational man have wanted? When I think back on my actions, I feel sick. On the other hand, her behavior was admirable. Even her sufferance of me was a sign of her kindness, for a day didn't pass when I, with some pretext or other, didn't impose on her. In a last-ditch effort to suffer the pain I deserved, I offered her a thousand dollars if she would sleep with me just one night. "You must be mad," was her reply. "Ten thousand," I said. "Ten thousand just to sleep with me?" she said. "Just for one night, what do you say?" She hesitated, which was all that I needed. "You were actually tempted," I said, and whipped off the disguise. "See? I'm no seducer, but your husband." When she saw it was me she rose from her chair and, saying nothing, not a single word, fled the house.

She joined a group of women, who having left their homes and having no places of their own, wandered in the mountains, worshipping Diana, hating men, and living off roots and berries and what animals they could kill. I despaired of ever seeing her again and devoted myself to self-pity. I told anyone who would listen pathetic tales of my attempts to cook, clean, and wash. I became famous as a hopeless case. At last, I sent Procris a message in which I pleaded for forgiveness. I confessed that I was a sinner of the first order and that were I in her shoes I would have gone for the thousand without a second's thought. My message must have eased some of Procris' hurt and given her some measure of satisfaction, because she came back to me, ready to take up our marriage again. And as if coming back were not in itself enough of a gift, she brought a hunting dog and a javelin.

The dog, whose name was Lelaps, was a fabulous animal. Procris and I would sit behind the house, sometimes for hours, enthralled by his beauty. Then it happened that tragedy struck the town where we were living. An enormous wild boar had come down from the hills and ravaged the herds of the local farmers. People were terrified and bolted their doors even during the day. Just the bravest young men went out and only to spread nets around the fields. But it didn't work. The monster leapt over the nets and dodged the traps set for him. And when the others in town set their dogs on his trail, they might as well have been following birds in the air. All this time Lelaps, sensing something was wrong, strained against his leash, eager to go. I was reluctant to turn him loose, fearing some harm would come to him, although with his speed it was impossible to imagine what difficulties he might encounter.

As soon as I let him go, he was out of sight, leaving only a thin trail of dust. I climbed to the top of a nearby hill to watch Lelaps chase the boar, and it was an amazing sight: the boar circling or zigzagging back and forth with Lelaps right on his heels. And each time it seemed that Lelaps had him, the boar would double away, leaving Lelaps snapping at empty air. Again and again it seemed that the dog had the boar in the grip of his jaws only to lose him. I had my javelin and, while I was getting set to hurl it, looked down a moment to make sure I had the proper grip. When I looked up, I saw something that still astonishes me: two marble statues in a field, one being chased, the other chasing. It must have been the gods' will that neither the dog nor the boar should lose.

Procris and I were more in love than I could believe possible. The moments of our passion kept spinning out of reach, drawing us on. Whether looking out over the wide valley, or sitting in front of the fire on rainy days, or wandering along the creek bank on sunlit afternoons, we yearned for each other. The days were not long enough. We were still young and each day brought with it a vague excitement, a sense that we were speeding toward a brilliant destiny. Back then, I still loved hunting, so when the sun rose I went off to the woods with nothing but the javelin that Procris had given me. I thought of nothing but pleasing her, of coming back with just enough game. Often, on my way home, I would lie down exhausted in some shady place and woo the breeze from the deep valleys. To better lure it into the open, I gave it a name. "Aura," I said, "cool me off. With your cold breath, comfort me, relax me, make me human again." And because I thought I was alone, I would go on, "Aura, my dear, my darling, drape your long body over mine; please, Aura, come to me now." One morning, a neighbor overheard me and assumed Aura was a girl I was in love with, and ran off to whisper in Procris' ear of my infidelity. And Procris, no doubt remembering what I had done to her in the past, believed what she heard. She cursed her fate and railed against the fickleness of men. What had she done to deserve such misery? Why were the gods treating her so? I imagine she marched nervously from room to room in her nightgown, her dark hair uncombed and wild-looking, her face pale, and all because of a neighbor's maliciousness, the mention of a mere name, the name of no one. Then she would sit a moment, collect her thoughts, and begin to doubt what she heard. She needed evidence. She would have to catch me in the act.

The next morning at the crack of dawn, I went hunting again. I knew nothing of the unfortunate rumor that had been torturing Procris and hunted with my usual fervor. When I lay down in the shade, exhausted, I called for a reviving breeze. "Aura," I said, "if I ever needed you, it is now." And as if in answer I heard a deep sigh. "Aura, come now," I cried. A few leaves rustled and a low bough shook. I thought it was a wild boar and let fly the javelin. This time I heard a cry of pain. It was Procris. I rushed to where she lay doubled over, trying to pull the spear from her breast. A huge poppy of blood stained the dull clothes she had worn to disguise herself. I did my best to stop the flow of blood, but it was no use. I held her in my arms and begged her not to leave me. She was breathing with difficulty, but managed in a soft, heaving voice to speak. "Please, Cephalus," she said, "if you love me at all as I love you—and my love for you has killed me—never allow Aura into our bedroom." So that was it. In a moment Procris was limp in my arms and her expressionless eyes were fixed on nothing.

II
CEPHALUS & BETTY

It was Aristotle in the *Problemata* who first connected melancholy with the making of beauty. But it is doubtful that Aristotle would have anticipated the sadness of Cephalus finding its way into poems. For months after the death of Procris, Cephalus mourned. He forgot about hunting and sat at a table, wrestling with the patterns and sounds of words. Often, late at night, one could hear his voice float through the air of the sleeping town. In the dark of her father's house, Betty heard the sorrowful strophes accompanied by the periodic strumming of a lyre and was moved to tears. She felt a deep connection with Cephalus' poems. Desire for an unimaginable order had set her adrift within herself and only when she heard his poems was she able to stop. In the radiance of those particular moments, she experienced an uplift in which all things were suddenly clear. She was no longer a vagrant in the enormous solitude that had been her life. Her days were not lived by someone not fully known, someone whose features were blurred, a twin of herself alive in a distant mirror. Like everyone else in town, she knew of Cephalus' tragedy, but unlike the others she did not blame him. Through listening to his poems, her life began to make sense. The energy of its progression, the routine of its inwardness, became a cloudless narrative, an irre-

ducible invention of the gods. Cephalus' poems made her
happy, and she could look back on her life without bitter-
ness or shame.

And this was not easy, for Betty's father believed that
money was the surest way to show love. During her ado-
lescence when he thought his daughter was growing away
from him, he would leave a hundred-dollar bill under her
pillow. The next day she would slip it into his jacket
pocket when he was not looking. Frustrated, he tried forcing the money on Betty by shoving it into her blouse as he
chased her around his air-conditioned backyard. Her refusal of his money was seen as a refusal of his love and he
dropped her from his will. This annoyed the ever-watchful
gods, who shortened his arms by several inches. Betty's
mother ran away to another town when Betty was still an
infant. Living alone in a roach-infested room, she would
take to the streets at night, swinging huge bags under her
arms, looking for things to pick up. When she died of
heart failure, she weighed five hundred pounds and was
worth five million dollars.

Poor Betty! It is no wonder poetry came to her rescue.
Anything that shed a kind light on the dark text of her
days and nights was welcome. Anything that promised to
fill the emptiness of the future had to be pursued. Knowing
that Cephalus walked the woods in search of inspiration,
Betty went and posted herself where he might see her.
But Cephalus was so caught up in his thoughts it wasn't
until Betty's fifth trip to the woods that he discovered her.
She was standing in the shade and—to quote a great
writer describing the first time he laid eyes on his love—
"she seemed to have been spontaneously generated there,
among the watchful trees, with the silent completeness of

a mythological manifestation." Heavy vines combed by an amber light hung down on all sides, flower clusters like handfuls of white dust dotted the forest floor. She stood with her feet turned slightly outward like a ballerina's and her long, cream-colored legs disappeared into a tan skirt just above the knees. Over a white blouse with a tiny round collar, she wore a green cardigan which hung open. Her short auburn hair was streaked with blond. There was something soft and vulnerable about her gaze that implied a readiness to sympathize. Suddenly, Cephalus caught himself and remembered Procris. He turned to walk away. "Please, don't go yet," Betty said, "let's talk about it." For a moment Cephalus was confused. "Talk about what?" he asked. "The terrible hold the past has on the present," said Betty.

After he told her the story that she already knew and she took his hand in hers, and after he looked up and encountered again the mild look in her eyes, Cephalus thought that perhaps the time of his mourning had come to an end. He led Betty to his house and into the very bedroom that Procris begged him never to take Aura, and they stayed there for days. Released from the woeful claims of their histories—Cephalus from the death of Procris, Betty from the moneyed attention of her father— they fell into a life of domestic calm and happiness. The poems of Cephalus changed. He now talked wistfully about shadows lengthening across a lawn, about the autumnal smell of burning leaves, about the light and stillness of particular evenings. He relinquished himself to those momentary pleasures that inevitably make us sad when we try to give them weight and permanence. He was getting older, but he was also a more tolerant and understanding husband than he had ever been. The gods who once intervened on behalf of Betty were pleased. Only Diana, loyal to the memory of Procris, was unhappy. She vowed to take vengeance on Betty.

One evening at dinner while Betty was praising an especially moving poem Cephalus had just written, Diana swung into action. Betty immediately began to change. As she spoke, her skin turned gradually darker and rougher. Her eyes widened into sad, watery brown orbs that edged out the white. Her words became slurred, and suggested, in their diminishing clarity, the first tentative sounds of a young elephant. It was a transformation that silenced Cephalus and had Betty suddenly on her feet. "I don't deserve this," she said. "Nothing I've done deserves this. I'm being punished and I've committed no crime. All I did was try to make you happy. Cephalus, hold me, tell me you'll love me no matter what. Tell me you'll get a doctor in to look at me." Within moments, however, her speech had given way to the trumpeting blasts of a fully grown female, blasts that embodied her terror of the unfortunate metamorphosis. Betty's nose lengthened into a trunk and her ears bloomed into enormous leathery flags, but from the waist down she was intact. "My god, Betty," Cephalus said, "you're turning into an elephant." Betty's legs wobbled under the weight of her suddenly immense upper body, and she had to sit. "I don't think a doctor's going to do much good," said Cephalus.

For the gods, of course, it was business as usual. That there are struggles on earth never to be resolved or loves that will never know peace is only of passing interest to them. Misfortunes happen, shades are lowered on every life. Even tonight, if you go down the right street, you may see Betty with her long, delicate legs almost hidden by the great bulk of her upper body, and Cephalus sitting, forever stunned by the gross, magisterially still creature that faces him, proof that the power of the gods to change the shapes of things is boundless.

Drogo

THE LIGHT THAT STREAMED IN THE windows was a summer light. The curtains billowed as if a couple of ghosts were wrestling inside them. The walls were white. The rug was pale green with a pink border. Three straightback chairs waited to be filled. "Drogo," I said, and Drogo, with his head buried in his hands, appeared across the room in one of the chairs. His spare, absolutely straight dark hair hung down over his bony fingers. "Drogo, it's good to see you again." But the feeling was not mutual. He looked at me and said, "I don't like being trotted out like this whenever the mood strikes you. It makes me feel cheap." He jumped up and started walking in small circles. His head was bent and his hands were clasped behind his back.

I had known him for years. His father, a lieutenant in

the Italian Army, was stationed on the eastern frontier and rarely came home. His mother, Maria V., was my best friend and urged me to treat Drogo like a son. She would invite me to their house and the three of us would sit in her small overheated flat and play cards or I would read to them from books I loved. Gradually, I assumed a greater and greater role in bringing him up. I sometimes forgot that he was someone else's son and believed it was I who had given him life, which, to a certain extent, I had. Drogo's behavior was determined by my own needs at particular times. He was given to fits of despondency, sudden moments of hilarity, shifts of feeling that were perplexing and disruptive to everyone but me. Since they were brought on, I now realize, to keep me from the kind of boredom I usually experienced with others, I had no complaints.

Increasingly, I felt the urge to travel and I took Drogo. We wintered in Rome, where he had an abortive affair with the beautiful Nicola C. We summered in Cuernavaca, where he fascinated the brilliant Octavio P. And always, I thought, despite his ups and downs, he was essentially happy and, what is more important, happy to be with me. I did not know that he found his life disordered, unpredictable, and confusing, nor did I suspect that he longed for another life. Clearly, the good times I had on these excursions blinded me to the truth. I took my authority— or I should say my authorship since he seemed, in a sense, my creation—too much for granted. Still, I found it hard to believe that the life I had chosen for him, one that gave me such pleasure, should be the source of his pain.

I lit a cigarette and leaned forward. "Drogo," I said, "didn't you like Mexico? I read you *Sir Gawain and the*

Green Knight, The Green Huntsman, Green Mansions,
and the works of Henry Green. And over the steep green
mountains the sky was dotted with small puffs of cloud
that were being drawn rapidly away. Don't you remember
the mornings when waves of tropical mist would keep
rolling and spreading around us?"

Drogo sat down. His face had the beautiful, peaceful
immunity of stone.

"Think back to Rome," I said, "when I read you *Rome
and a Villa, Roman Fever,* and *A Time in Rome.* Remember the heat and haze of that August? Even the grass
in the Borghese Gardens seemed to drowse, and the ocean
at Ostia was so bright it seemed to set the sky on fire."

The curtains had stopped billowing. The inpouring light
had a faint yellowish tint. Drogo leaned back. "I wish this
would stop," he said.

"What about that summer in Maine when we took the
boat out in the gray waters of twilight and how silent it
was as we moved by ghostly piers and narrow windowless
houses crouched along the shore? And what about the sky,
those low clouds coming down from the North, scattered
like pages torn from an unfinished book? That was the
summer I read you nothing. Don't you remember?"

Drogo took a file from his pocket and began filing his
nails.

"And there was Salt Lake," I said, "and the poet whose
back was tattooed with dozens of tiny portraits of herself,
a creased, decaying album that threatened to take over her
buttocks and legs. Surely you remember?"

Drogo would have none of it. My reminiscences fell
on deaf ears. The wind started up again, punching the
curtains into the room. "What about the pool in Tampa,

the one with the Teddy bear? Or the man in Toronto who stood waist deep in the ground?" Drogo smirked, and my thoughts returned to the poetess of Salt Lake City. I had always found her attractive, someone I could work with. She was nothing like Drogo; she believed in my enterprise and wanted to help.

It had gotten dark. A sea breeze blew into the room. A freakish sound glided through the trees, something between a hum and a scream. Far off, there was thunder. I was anxious to busy myself with something else, something brighter and happier. I sent Drogo off, lit another cigarette, leaned back, and pondered what my next move would be. Let us say that while I sat there the storm cleared up, that moonlight silvered the walks and tipped the trees with white. Let us say that the neighbors were asleep and in front of my house stood a woman in a faded Carmen evening gown and ash-blue boa that she trailed behind her. When she saw me she smiled.

"I was just thinking of you," I said.

She stepped into the living room. "Things haven't been going well," she said. "So many golden opportunities have slipped away. So many days down the drain." And turning away, she took off her dress, her bra, and her panties. That evening, as she stared at the wall, I studied her, every face that was hers, and I think she wept, wept for me, for herself, and for what would become of us.

The Killer Poet

YOU ALL KNOW THE STORY OF Stanley R., that he murdered his parents for no reason, and never repented, that it happened in another country, the country of my childhood, youth, and early manhood, a small, mostly mountainous place to the south that ran narrowly for a few hundred miles along the Atlantic. Palm trees lined the boulevards, and grass grew between the slabs of concrete. Chickens, cows, and horses wandered untended through the neighborhoods. The air smelled of urine and burning charcoal and fat frying. Sunlight glittered on the spikes of broken glass set in the cement walls surrounding even the houses of the poor.

It was a country that had never won a war; the monuments to generals in the countless town squares commemorated defeats—the surest indicator of how the people there felt toward themselves. They had no national pride, and personal pride, depending on circumstances, seemed either pointless or comic. Nevertheless, they were not a people who liked being reminded of their impoverishment, nor did they tolerate anyone willing to overlook it. It was a poor place for literature. So, it was ironic of the government to establish a National Literature Board and doubly ironic to assign it the task of awarding a prize for the best book published each year. Stanley and I were suspicious that any good would come of such a committee. After all, he and I were the only writers the country had. We were convinced that the course of our nation's poetry would be the course of our own. We were also convinced that poets as revolutionary as we were would never receive official acknowledgment.

Stanley's parents were middle class. His father sold men's wear in a store he was part owner of. His mother stayed home, tending the house, which was small and square. Beautifully situated on the edge of a rich landowner's estate, it had access to rolling lawns, flower beds, and stands of trees. It was plainly, even sparsely, furnished, and there were reproductions of Impressionist paintings on the walls.

Of his parents, Stanley was more like his mother. He had her dark hair, long nose, and brown eyes. He also had her seeming indifference to everything, which must have masked an infinite curiosity. Her beauty was more austere than his and there was an aimlessness about her which Stanley did not have. Stanley's father was stockily built and sported a small black mustache. He was standoffish and made his disapproval of Stanley known as often as possible by narrowing his eyes at him, by shrugging, or, most rashly, by leaving the room when Stanley entered.

Stanley looked more like a poet than anyone I'd ever met. His uncombed hair hung down over his glasses and he was always wetting his lips with his tongue. His speech was unusual. I remember his saying once that snow was the pointed and overwhelming eloquence of cold, another time that fire was the concentrated redundance of heat. One sad evening I heard him say that the soft syllables of his mother's voice were the diminished radiance of love. The range, the possibilities, the seemingly inexhaustible fertility of his imagination were astonishing. There were times a few of us would watch and listen as Stanley, sitting in a cone of yellow light, his thin fingers holding the sheets on which he had written, read his poems in that high-pitched nasal voice of his. Clearly, he was one of the chosen, as different from us as we were from those who had no interest in poetry. As soon as he finished reading, he would close his eyes and be elsewhere, unreachable, and we, his enthralled audience, basked in the mythic place his poems had created.

When I left the country to continue my education in one of the great centers of learning to the north, Stanley and I wrote to one another—he about the slow progress of his verse, I about my growing interest in criticism. I wanted news from home, but Stanley had little to give. He rarely went out. He said the weather was disagreeable and he was increasingly bored by people. What Stanley wanted to hear from me, he never said, but our correspondence over the next few years waned and finally died.

When I returned, I didn't look him up, fearing that our old intimacy would be entirely gone, that there might be little to say, and that he would disapprove of my newly acquired worldliness. For whatever reason, I felt I had to know everything or at least appear to know everything. The more I feared seeming foolish, the more fixed was my mask of sophistication. Still, I did ask about Stanley, but nobody knew anything. I was told he still lived with his parents and never went out. It was assumed that he had given up writing, that his brilliant promise had come to naught. But just because no one had seen Stanley's poetry, it didn't follow that he'd given up writing. All that could be said was that he preferred to remain hidden. Poets in those days, in the absence of anything to be gained materially from their labors, longed for praise, and if they didn't get it they settled for understanding. But not too much understanding, since it might cause self-scrutiny and, consequently, doubt. Some pursued women whose availability offered them a reprieve from their failure to sway the muse. Stanley, however, cultivated distance. He had no desire to be rescued or reassured.

There was a day, not long after I got back, when I could have spoken to Stanley. It was in the middle of summer. A dark cloud from the eastern mountains swept over the city and cast a pall, a weird half-light, everywhere. A stifling stillness made the world seem like a sunken place where things lived a single moment infinitely extended. I walked in the yellow-gray light, among the shining trees and bushes. Finches and warblers whirled about me like bright confetti. I began to hum. And then I saw Stanley nearby, looking up into the branches of a tree. The tilt of his head, his obvious concentration revealed a religious aspect to him that surprised and delighted me. But I didn't go over and say hello. Something held me back. Perhaps part of me would not be deceived and sensed that Stanley was really troubled. This was the time, it turns out, that he started to think of murdering his parents.

About a year later, when my first book was published, I was put on the National Literature Board. Although I was dubious of the honor, I accepted, thinking that I might do some good for literature. I was young, but by no means unsure of my powers of judgment. I had the flashy convictions that now seem the staple of all young critics. I was nervous and talkative, and I believed what I said about literature mattered.

The Board met in a small fishing town up the coast from the capital. Not easily reached, it only contributed to the secrecy of the meetings, which were held in the spring when the rains were heavy and the air reeked, more than usual, of fish. Gulls posted themselves on the edges of the rotting wharves, on the roof peaks of fishhouses, on the barrels of brine. Everything glittered with fishscales. The inhabitants, who wore ragged clothing and coughed a lot, lived in row houses just wide enough for a door and window. They came out in the early evening to smoke and talk.

The building in which the meetings were held creaked in the lightest wind. The meeting room itself was cavernous and wooden and poorly lit by an ornate chandelier that cast a yellow varnished light everywhere. As the youngest and newest member of the Board, I had not known what to expect. We stood behind our chairs, placed on both sides of a long table. Along the walls, in armchairs that were set in large boxes of clear plastic, sat the deceased previous chairmen of the Board. Gray-faced, sleepy-eyed, they were the perennial backdrop of the gatherings. With the push of a button, their recorded voices, like a chorus of nobles or bankers, called out from the other world, "Will the meeting please come to order."

There was a certain honor attached to being a member of the Board, which meant that an air of self-congratulation colored the opening discussions. Members would refer parenthetically to their own work, suggesting it was a standard against which all works might be judged.

Normally, crumpled paper would litter the floor and smoke fill the air, complaints of spiritual aimlessness would be levelled at society, and threats to refuse the prize to anyone were frequent. But this year it was different. The Board, having read the submitted volumes before the final meeting, was in agreement. One book, though printed in a very limited edition, was far and away the best. It was Stanley's first and long-awaited book of poems.

The Board members by and large were failed poets and fiction writers who had stumbled into criticism. So it was no surprise some of them in reading Stanley's poems were able to overlook their most remarkable feature. There was mention made of the poetry's "eerie solemnity," of its "mystical consistency," but nothing was said about Stanley's having murdered his parents, even though he made no attempt to hide the fact. On the contrary, he made constant allusions to it, wrote about death's fecundity, its conclusive energy, its power to liberate and transform.

One of the members who opposed giving Stanley the prize did so on grounds that had nothing to do with the book's disclosures. "The book is too thin," he said. He insisted that poets were advocates of absence, refusal, and negative quantities, that too many of them believed their power to be directly proportional to what they left out of their work. "For them," he concluded, "the mere lifting of a pen satisfies the claims of their calling."

Another, getting closer to the point, admitted that he admired Stanley's honesty. "But," he said, "to reward him for sincerity might seem a way of excusing his crimes, just as dealing exclusively with his crimes would be overlooking the accomplishment of his work."

The problem was both absurd and difficult—how to recognize Stanley's remarkable ability and, at the same time, condemn his hideous crimes. Whatever we chose to do would have to make moral sense, or poetry would be subject to even greater ridicule and public censure than it already was. I was torn. I wanted a compromise, something that would satisfy everyone. I shook my head in disbelief that Stanley could have done such a thing. I wondered if I had ever really known him. Then, without realizing what came over me, I suddenly stood up and suggested that we not give the prize. "I think we should convict and execute him," I said. I pointed out that suicidal poets had blazed a trail showing how easily death could validate art. I went on to say that Stanley would be a martyr for poetry, a special saint, that his immortality would be ensured. I felt a little like Judas in taking such extreme measures to speed up the immortality of a friend, but I consoled myself by knowing that he would be spared the humiliation of institutional acceptance. After all, what kind of poet is it who wins official approval during his lifetime!

After I had spoken there was a moment of stunned silence and I thought my proposal was done for. Then several Board members shot to their feet and, instead of denouncing me, voiced their approval.

When I called Stanley and told him that the National Literature Board wanted to meet with him and would send a limousine to bring him to our meeting place, he was not only willing to come but delighted at the prospect of seeing me again. This, of course, filled me with sadness. There wouldn't be much time for us to renew our friendship.

I stood outside in the gray weather, waiting for him, waiting to see if he'd changed in appearance. Maybe I would not recognize him. Maybe he would be violent. Gulls and man-o'-war birds drifted overhead on the cold, withering wind. My collar was turned up and my hands were in my pockets. I felt like a gangster.

When he arrived, we shook hands and I led him inside. I was surprised to discover that his body had thickened and that his hair had turned almost entirely gray. There were dark rings under his eyes. He looked beaten. "Stanley," I said, "what I am about to say would be difficult enough, but our being old friends makes it doubly difficult." The absurdity of the situation came crashing down on me, and I wanted to tell Stanley that it was a joke, that a mistake had been made, and that he should go home.

"I know what you are going to say," he answered. "I've thought a lot about it. You're going to say that my book deserves the prize, but that it's much too disturbing, and that you brought me here to dispense justice. You're going to execute me."

"Then you understand," I said.

"Yes," he said.

The rest is history. Everyone knows that while Stanley wrote his last words, the rest of us prayed, that while he walked to his death, some of us wished we could join him, and that just moments before I pulled the trigger, ending his life, Stanley leaned over and thanked me.

STANLEY'S LAST WORDS

This letter written on the eve of my execution will, I hope, put the crimes I committed in a perspective uncomplicated by suspicion or hatred. I am not what I appear. My so-called crimes, though certain to define me for some, were in the service of a calling that exceeded everything else. I loved poetry. It was my single passion. I am not sure why, but I was never much drawn to people. Either they frightened me or didn't interest me. Still, my distance from them was not, I think, in itself contemptible. I know there are those who would dispute this, but there is an untouched, untold, altogether unreached part of me that stands condemned along with the more impetuous side of my nature.

Of my early years there is little to say. I would leaf through the family album, trying to discover in the frozen expressionless faces of my ancestors something of myself. Sometimes I read, but without sympathy or admiration for victim or hero. I could not concentrate. I thought only of being a poet. Long afternoons I stared from my window across the elm-shaded lawn and was filled with languor. My perception of the world was muted and secret. I considered myself a fortunate but distant witness to what went on. I took pleasure in the green damp that soiled the

air and the swift clouds that ruined the edge of sight. My
enjoyment, however, was forced to mingle—at first grudg-
ingly, then submissively—with my lack of energy. The
result was that I would spend days on my back, lost in a
gravity of unsurpassable sweetness. Though my medita-
tions were filled with the self-regarding pomp of adoles-
cence, something important was taking hold of me—the
privileged and ponderous assessment, for the first time, of
my own mortality. The beauty and mystery of death beck-
oned, and I began to write. My anguished humming into
the empty corridors of the future, my plangent dialogues
with absence, were all that sustained me. I did not go to
school, nor did I grant my parents in any day more than a
few minutes of my time. The silence I inflicted on them
was brooding, but never reproachful. I was bored. But
boredom became illumination. The consideration of suicide became my one joy. I lay around the house feeling the
pointlessness of pleasure, the emptiness of enchantment.
Then it occurred to me that the idea of a single victim was
too constraining a notion, and on behalf of my imagination I made the transition from thoughts of suicide to
those of homicide. I was maturing rapidly, and I reasoned
that I had less to lose by killing others than by killing
myself.

My feelings about my parents were imprecise and dis-
connected, and lacked an intensity that suggested the possibility of murdering them. The truth is I rarely thought
about them. Though there were moments I saw my mother
in the kitchen, framed against the window, and the beautiful severity of her profile thrilled me, such moments were
ephemeral. Briefly caught in the inflowing light, she
seemed to possess the serene autonomy of neo-classical

sculpture. My mother always seemed on the verge of sleep. By mid-afternoon she was already looking forward to night. Repose was all she longed for. When I saw her at night—those times I would sneak into my parents' bedroom—it never occurred to me that she might be meeting an imaginary lover in the secret dark of her soul or dreaming of anything even remotely connected with sex. On the contrary, since so much of her life seemed dominated by a certain coldness and immobility, I got the impression that she would not mind being dead. It struck me that I could be an agent of change and give her the death she longed for. I was so moved one night by her languid beauty that I could not but follow her into the drowsing garden behind the house. Let me say, in case there is any doubt, that my motives were pure. I was not angry with my mother, and in respect to everything but her marriage to my father I found her faultless.

I saw her walking in her nightgown through the garden to the lake, where she stood covered with phosphorescence. A deep enveloping haze swept over her and she lay down, feeling, I am sure, like oblivion's beautiful sister adrift in the swells of vague light. Seeing her so made me mourn in advance the death that awaited her. My mother, who died at my hands without a cry, who thought of me in that veiled night perhaps as a lover come to take her away, never knew in those last moments that I heard a mournful music and saw her already asleep in the shadow of the ages. I exulted in the miracle of her death. I don't think she ever saw the knife, but if she did, in that terminal instant, it must have been as a streak of moonlight. All around us I felt the air of summer flee the scene. I rose from my knees and went to the garden, where I lay alone and thought of the poem I would write, one that would do justice to the cold enigma of my mother's beauty. I lay there a long time under the moon, and in the corners of the garden the enormous cabbages, the sleeping eggplants took upon themselves the ancient sheen of night. An air of fertility formed an invisible crown of fullness everywhere, which is why, I suppose, I conceived a poem not about what I intended but about tomatoes, fennel, squash, and the buried inverted obelisks of carrot and parsnip.

I killed my mother before I killed my father because I did not want to be misinterpreted. Had I killed my father first, people would say it was because I wanted to sleep with my mother. This way I could not be thought more complex than I was. But why I bothered to go ahead and kill my father when I wasn't especially fond of him, I don't know. Perhaps I feared his reprisals, perhaps I wanted to spare him the anguish of discovering his loss and his having, thenceforth, to live in it. I leave the answer to the psychologists and searchers for motives. That I was a dreamy, poetical child, you already know, but that I found no encouragement in my preoccupation is something else. Still, that hardly explains why I murdered the old man, nor does the fact that he was ashamed of me, nor even that his loathing of me gave him pleasure and, in fact, obsessed him. I suppose I was free to kill him. As his son, I was his prisoner; as his prisoner, I was being punished. And because I was being punished, I was relieved of guilt. In other words, my deprivation was my freedom. Or, to take my reasoning one step further: by making me feel that I had paid for any crime that I might commit, my father was complicitous in his own death.

When I rose from the garden and the lush untroubled

thoughts of the poem I would write, I went to my parents'
bedroom, where my father, despite his mustache, his grizzled hair, and thin, creased face, lay curled like a child. I
lifted his pajama-clad body and carried him to the birdbath and put an end to his life. If he struggled, I do not
remember. I remember only a kind of uplift. Inspired by a
radiance hitherto unknown to me, I felt blissfully relieved,
and images endless and singing suddenly flooded my mind.
When I held my father's head under the water of the
birdbath, I was in another world. And when I left his
sopping body hanging half out of the concrete bowl and
backed away, I thought of myself, finally, without inhibi-
tions, as a poet. I was more than a biographical instant,
more than a blur in the calculus of events. I became part
of the nation of poets moving across a great plain, reciting
their poems forever.

I suppose it was this sudden exhilaration that sent me
after my dog with an ax. Though I was never on trial for
killing Bob Kahn—that was his name—who had eyes so
sad he seemed always on the verge of tears, it was he who
not only interested me most, but whom I loved more than
anybody. The revisions and shifts of feeling I had for him
were the compendium, no doubt, of all that I repressed in
terms of people. He was so good that I turned him into an
angel. I like to imagine that he sits now at the feet of God,
and God, every so often, reaches down and pats his head,
and Bob Kahn wags his tail that glitters with thousands of
tiny stars. Was it a terrible thing that I found him a better
master, that I spared him the humiliation of serving others
whose priorities in matters of friendship lay entirely with
people?

Clearly I am not a bad person. If I seem hidden or

guarded, it is because I never understood how candor benefited the imagination. I chose not to shed light but to embody darkness, not to reveal order, but to withhold it. I was alive with the negative certainty of my passion. Each day I luxuriated in the possession of myself. My sight was always turned inward. The winds, the tides, the distant lights I found there were the vague signs of a kingdom where the hills were blue marble and the sky a vast mirror. It was the place I wanted to reach. I would close my eyes and the humming of possibilities would begin and I would be driven into a frenzy of expectation. I would approach my kingdom, as I do now. O proximity of nothingness, O language eager to enter the measures of timelessness, forgive me.

A Note on the Type

The text of this book was set in Times Roman, a face designed by Stanley Morison for *The Times* (London) and first introduced by that newspaper in 1932. Among typographers and designers of the twentieth century, Stanley Morison has been a strong forming influence, as typographical adviser to the English Monotype Corporation, as director of two distinguished English publishing houses, and as a writer of sensibility, erudition, and keen practical sense.

Composed by Maryland Linotype
Composition Co., Inc., Baltimore, Maryland
Printed and bound by The Maple-Vail
Book Manufacturing Group,
York, Pennsylvania

Designed by Iris Weinstein